# You're a Privileged Woman.

INTRODUCING
### *PAGES & PRIVILEGES™*.

It's our way of thanking you for buying
our books at your favorite retail store.

## GET ALL THIS FREE

### WITH JUST ONE PROOF OF PURCHASE:

◆ Hotel Discounts up to 60% at home and abroad

◆ Travel Service - Guaranteed lowest published
airfares plus 5% cash back on tickets

◆ $25 Travel Voucher

◆ Sensuous Petite Parfumerie collection ($50 value)

◆ Insider Tips Letter with sneak previews of
upcoming books

◆ Mystery Gift (if you enroll before 6/15/95)

*You'll get a FREE personal card, too.
It's your passport to all these benefits– and to
even more great gifts & benefits to come!*

*There's no club to join. No purchase commitment. No obligation.*

# As a Privileged Woman,
## you'll be entitled to all
## these *Free Benefits*.
## And *Free Gifts*, too.

To thank you for buying our books, we've designed an exclusive FREE program called *PAGES & PRIVILEGES*™. You can enroll with just one Proof of Purchase, and get the kind of luxuries that, until now, you could only read about.

## BIG HOTEL DISCOUNTS

**A privileged woman stays in the finest hotels**. And so can you—at up to 60% off! Imagine standing in a hotel check-in line and watching as the guest in front of you pays $150 for the same room that's only costing you $60. Your *Pages & Privileges* discounts are good at Sheraton, Marriott, Best Western, Hyatt and thousands of other fine hotels all over the U.S., Canada and Europe.

## FREE DISCOUNT TRAVEL SERVICE

**A privileged woman is always jetting to romantic places.** When you fly, just make one phone call for the lowest published airfare at time of booking—<u>or double the difference back</u>! PLUS—

you'll get a $25 voucher to use the first time you book a flight AND <u>5% cash back on every ticket you buy thereafter through the travel service</u>!

## *She was* **not** *in denial.*

Abby had no idea *what* she was in.

But trouble came instantly to mind.

She had no business getting involved with Reed Mackintosh. Not in the way she was considering. Reed was only trying to help her and her family start over, feel comfortable, in Winston. It was her own fault if his help, his comfort, was making her think silly thoughts.

And, oh, she did feel silly. And foolish. And giddy.

And scared.

Reed was Winston's main womanizer. A handsome, lovable, devilish...womanizer. Abby knew that. Had *always* known that. Yet she couldn't deny her desire. Feelings that took her very breath.

Yes, there was definitely something special between her and Reed.

Abby just wasn't sure what it was!

Dear Reader,

Spring is the perfect time to celebrate the joy of new romance. So get set to fall in love as Silhouette Romance brings you six new wonderful books.

Blaine O'Connor is a *Father in the Making* in Marie Ferrarella's heartwarming FABULOUS FATHERS title. When this handsome bachelor suddenly becomes a full-time dad, he's more than happy to take a few lessons in child rearing from pretty Bridgette Rafanelli. Now he hopes to teach Bridgette a thing or two about love!

Love—Western style—begins this month with a delightful new series, WRANGLERS AND LACE. Each book features irresistible cowboys and the women who tame their wild hearts. The fun begins with *Daddy Was a Cowboy* by Jodi O'Donnell.

In Carolyn Zane's humorous duet, SISTER SWITCH, twin sisters change places and find romance. This time around, sister number two, Emily Brant, meets her match when she pretends sexy Tyler Newroth is her husband in *Weekend Wife*.

Also this month, look for *This Man and This Woman*, an emotional story by Lucy Gordon about a wedding planner who thinks marriage is strictly business—until she meets a dashing Prince Charming of her own. And don't miss *Finally a Family*, Moyra Tarling's tale of a man determined to win back his former love—and be a father to the child he never knew he had. And Margaret Martin makes her debut with *Husband in Waiting*.

Happy Reading!

Anne Canadeo
Senior Editor

Please address questions and book requests to:
Silhouette Reader Service
U.S.: 3010 Walden Ave., P.O. Box 1325, Buffalo, NY 14269
Canadian: P.O. Box 609, Fort Erie, Ont. L2A 5X3

# HUSBAND IN WAITING

## Margaret Martin

Silhouette
R O M A N C E™
Published by Silhouette Books
America's Publisher of Contemporary Romance

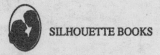

**SILHOUETTE BOOKS**

ISBN 0-373-19083-2

HUSBAND IN WAITING

Copyright © 1995 by Margaret Dobson Casey

Printed in U.S.A.

## MARGARET MARTIN

lives in Arkansas. When she isn't writing she enjoys sewing, travel and basic carpentry. She enjoys writing romances because they bring "a special kind of thrill. Two characters—a man and a woman—unfold before my eyes and often present more than a few surprises."

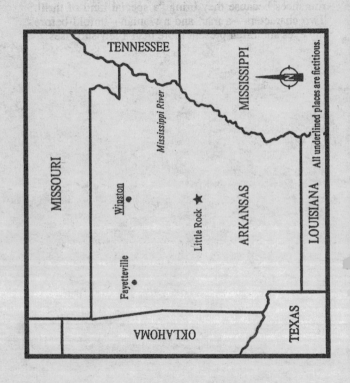

# Chapter One

Fourteen years ago she had shown him the door.

He wondered if she was still angry.

Reed Mackintosh also wondered if he was seeing things.

On his way to Charlie's Drugstore and Soda Fountain, he had paid no attention to the Saturday morning goings-on in the town square. But now he stood just inside the pharmacy gazing out of the plate-glass window at the woman across the way. A woman who looked remarkably like Abby Malone. A woman he hadn't expected to see in Winston ever again.

She turned a bit and a ray of sunlight glanced off her face and sent a memory shooting through him. Abby smiling. Abby laughing. And then she was turning away again.

Reed adjusted the venetian blinds for a better view. The slightest tingle teased the back of his neck, and he reached up to rub it away. In the August sunshine, a little girl alternately pranced and hopped first in front of, then alongside, the woman. The child's hair, and the mother's—he guessed that was the relationship—were a rich shade of brown, curling slightly and framing their faces.

Vaguely aware that Charlie had said something, Reed tried to remember the purpose of his visit.

"Look, Reed," Charlie Johnson said from behind the high counter, "I'd like to help you out here, but I'm a pharmacist and businessman, not a counselor, and this kid—well, he doesn't sound like the kind I could get much work out of."

"Sure you could," Reed assured him. "That's why I asked you, Charlie. You'd straighten him out in no time." He returned to his view of the courthouse lawn. Now mother and daughter were moving toward the old gazebo that stood just to the left of a willow. "Besides," Reed continued, "the kid turns sixteen in two weeks. That means a license. He could make deliveries for you after school and—"

"Will he have his own wheels?"

"Nope."

"Well, damn, Reed, you know what that'll do to my insurance."

"Yes, and I'm prepared to pick up the extra cost."

Charlie was standing beside him now. "Why?"

"Why?" Reed paused, noticing that Mavis, Charlie's waitress-clerk, was about to dust the same shelf for the third time, obviously to hear why he wanted Frankie to have this job. "Well, he's a good kid, and we just think—"

"Who is 'we'?" Charlie asked. "And if he's so wonderful, why isn't he working for you and your dad at Mackintosh?"

"He was. But the furniture business…well, it just wasn't his cup of tea." Reed was convinced that the kid would have dropped a cup of tea, too, but he didn't say so.

Problem was, Frankie couldn't seem to pick up one piece of furniture without slamming it into another piece of furniture. And they didn't dare let him in the plant. Reed didn't say that, either.

"But like I said—" Reed let his voice drop to a whisper so that Mavis would have to strain to overhear "—he's smart. And he's great around people. With just a minimum of attention, I think the kid will surprise you."

"Oh, I get it," Charlie said. "You wouldn't be grooming him for one of those Mackintosh scholarships, would you?"

"Not necessarily," Reed whispered. "He's a little young for that, but who knows? Right now, he just needs a job. His family's dirt-poor and he wants to help out." He leaned toward the platinum blond waitress and spoke considerably louder. "Isn't that right, Mavis?"

"Hey, anything you say, y'hear?" Mavis gave him an unabashed grin before she turned away and moved on to the next shelf.

"Well, let me think about it." Scratching the bald spot at the back of his head, Charlie went to greet another customer.

"I'd appreciate it," Reed said. Turning back to the window, he squinted into the sunlight. Maybe he just *wanted* the woman to be Abby. Maybe he just *wanted* the little girl to be Abby's little girl. If it was Abby, then where was her son? He would be almost fifteen or so by now. Reed searched the area around the gazebo, but he didn't see any kid he didn't know. Still...

He wasn't sure. All he knew was that his heart had begun to beat noticeably faster, just thinking about the possibility. Early morning shoppers, some strolling, some moving briskly on the sidewalk, passed in front of Charlie's. A few people waved or mouthed hellos to Reed, who nodded pleasantly to each one before turning his gaze again toward the courthouse.

She was wearing red slacks and a short-sleeved shirt. Sandals, too. Very petite...very nice...attractive. He had missed her. Those last words rose in his mind on a slow sigh.

The woman, whoever she was, sat on a bench with her child and began acquainting herself with the buildings on the square—or maybe reacquainting herself, he thought. Crossing one knee over the other, she leaned close to her daughter and pointed to, he guessed, the big red rooster atop the Co-Op building. The little girl squealed with laughter as the woman tickled her. Then Abby—he was almost positive it was Abby—leaned back and laughed, too.

She was a good mother. He could see that much in the way the little girl snuggled next to her and received a hug in return. A pleasant tightness pressed into his gut. He supposed he ought to go over there and just make sure, say hello, do something. Maybe they would like an ice-cream float from Charlie's soda fountain. He checked his watch. Maybe not, since it was only nine o'clock in the morning.

Reed heard the cash register close. Charlie held the door open for Theodora Walsh. "Come back now, hear? And tell your sister I'll stop by with her prescription on my way home this evening."

"Fine, Mr. Johnson. I thank you for your trouble."

Miss Walsh patted the silver-streaked bun at the back of her neck. She had worn it that way so long that Reed figured by this time her hair could probably get up every morning and march itself right into place without so much as a how-de-do from Theodora Walsh. He had to respect her, though. She'd given over forty no-nonsense years to the Winston public schools, retiring only last year and lived with her younger sister, Henrietta.

As she passed him, Reed gave her a polite smile. "Good morning, Miss Walsh. You're looking well."

Miss Walsh stopped in the doorway and eyed him for a moment before her lips tightened a little and she lifted her chin, sparing him an even tighter nod. "Mr. Mackintosh." It was more a statement than a greeting. As usual.

Reed didn't dare laugh.

He could never recall exactly why he inspired that particular reaction in Miss Walsh. He figured it had begun sometime around his sophomore year in high school. Something to do with her roses . . . and his motorcycle.

When she had gone, Charlie rejoined him at the window. "Oh, the pleasures of a misspent youth," he whispered.

Reed ignored the taunt. "Some people really know how to hold a grudge."

"Tire tracks across a front porch are, well . . . memorable."

"Come on, it wasn't that bad."

"You know, I think Miss Walsh feels about you the way a lot of folks in the South feel about the Civil War," Charlie persisted. "Hell, no, I ain't fergittin'—that's what a lot of them say. Don't you hear a lot of them say that, Reed?"

"The kid, Charlie. What about the kid?" Reed stared out the window again, letting Charlie have his fun, hoping it might put him in a receptive mood about Frankie.

"Look, maybe we could give it a try, Reed. Why don't you send the kid around. Maybe he could start by cleaning up a little, to see how it goes. But I want you to know up front that if it doesn't work out—"

"Yeah, right," Reed said. "I appreciate your trouble. Say, Charlie, take a look over at the gazebo. See anyone you know?" Charlie would remember. He, like Reed, had been a lifelong friend of Abby's.

"Guess I know just about everybody over there," Charlie declared with a shrug. "There's Clyde Barker and his two boys...Jennifer Smith and her dog, Amos...oh, and Abby Malone and her little girl, Molly."

Reed felt a momentary tightness in his throat. "You're certain? You know it's Abby?" he pressed, needing further assurance. She was just a former classmate, for God's sake. Even as the thought formed, he knew it wasn't the whole truth. Abby had never been just a classmate. Abby had always been . . . Abby.

"Of course it's her," Charlie said. "She and her two kids came in for ice cream late yesterday afternoon."

Reed let go of the blind. "Why didn't somebody tell me?"

Charlie shrugged. "You never asked. But your pop knew. Matter of fact, he's the one who told me they were coming. Said he had it straight from Abby's mother last week. Didn't he say anything?"

"Not a word." Damn that Ben. "Any idea how long they'll be in town?"

"Didn't you hear? Oh. Guess you didn't. She's back for good. Buying the Rollins place and—"

"Here? In Winston?"

Charlie shrugged and drifted back to the counter to help another customer. "Last I heard, that's where the Rollins place was. The corner of Melrose and—"

"Right." Reed rubbed his jaw. Maybe he would walk across the street and say hello. Then again, maybe he wouldn't. The last time he had spoken to her, she had told him to get lost. Permanently.

And last year, when Jason had died, hell, he'd been in Sacramento and hadn't even made it home in time for the funeral. The best he could do was a lousy card conveying his condolences. It hadn't seemed like much at the time. Now it seemed like nothing at all. Still, there was no way he could not go and see her.

"Bye, Charlie. See you around." Reed opened the door and stepped into the morning heat.

Abby was nowhere in sight.

"Well, ain't this a kick in the pants."

Ben Mackintosh had been saying that same thing ever since Abby could remember. Older, but still robust, Reed's father pushed away from his desk and stood.

"Abby Lindstrom. Is it really you?"

"It's really me. But make that Abby Malone." Abby wasn't at all surprised or disappointed when he came around the big oak desk and hugged her.

"I heard you were coming home," he said. "Saw your mother last week and she told me. Took you long enough. Thought maybe you'd forgotten where home was."

Abby welcomed his teasing the way she always had. Over the years his voice had aged to a rough, gravelly drawl. Too much brandy and too many cigars, Abby suspected. But she rather liked the evolution. He had put on a few pounds around the middle, which only gave him added distinction. Ben Mackintosh ran his hand through thick hair that had finally given in to the slightest graying and looked over her shoulder toward the door. "Did you bring your kids?"

"I left Molly at Mother's," she explained. "And Matthew's having his own private look around town...without his mother's interference."

"Ah." Ben nodded as if he understood only too well.

Abby herself was still trying to understand a son who didn't seem to want her around anymore.

"I took a chance you'd be here," she said. But Abby realized there was no risk at all. "Still coming into the office every Saturday morning, I see."

"Come hell or high water," he answered and then smiled. "Old habits die hard. How are you, Abigail?" he asked a little more soberly.

She took a seat near the office door and made herself comfortable on the rich leather upholstery. "Getting better, thank you."

"Well, sure you are. It'll just take time, that's all. And then you'll be good as—" He stopped and shook his head. "What the hell am I saying? I used to hate when people said that stuff to me. When my Edie died ... Good God, for the longest time I couldn't take a breath without hurting. You probably don't remember her, do you?"

"Of course I remember Mrs. Mackintosh."

Reed had turned fifteen the year his mother had died. Edie Mackintosh had made her husband and her son her life and no one had ever stood a chance of taking her place. Reed had never allowed anyone to get too close again. Certainly not her. Jason, maybe. But Jason was gone and . . .

For a moment, Abby clamped her jaw tightly to hold back the feeling. She didn't want to think about death and dying today. But neither did she want to appear unkind.

"You still miss her very much, don't you?" Abby said.

"Sure do. I still talk to that woman every day just as I did when she was alive." He gave Abby the slightest grin. "She listens about like she did back then, too."

Abby sighed her appreciation. This man had been good to her. And to her husband. Jason could never have become a doctor without his help. She felt a little guilty staying away so long, but Jason had never been especially interested in returning to Winston, not even for short visits, once he had made it through med school.

"Hear you're fixing up the Rollins place," Ben said.

Mother again, Abby thought. "Yes, and when I began to consider furnishings, I naturally thought of you."

"Well, I should certainly hope so." Sitting back in his chair, he tapped his fingers together. "We've got some pieces that would really show off that house. What did you have in mind?"

"I brought a lot of what I need from Little Rock," she began. "But I did see your Christmas catalog from last year and there's a bedroom suite I fell in love with."

"Don't tell me. Everlasting. Traditional walnut? Four-poster and highboy?"

Amazing. "How did you know?"

"Simple," he said easily. "It's *you*, Abigail."

"My mother told you," she said just as easily.

"Okay, okay. She mentioned it. But it really does suit you. That's Reed's baby, you know."

"He designed it?"

Ben nodded. "Came up with the line year before last. There's an armoire with beveled glass in the group, too. To be honest, I'm surprised it's done so well."

She wasn't surprised. Not at all. "I still have the desk he designed and built when we were seniors in high school—the one I received for coming up with the slogan for your fall ad campaign. Remember that?"

"'Course I do." Ben shook his head. "Good Lord, that was a long time ago. As I recall, that's when you decided to go after a degree in marketing."

"Right." Big dreams, she thought. But in her third year at university, Matthew had come along and instantly put that particular dream on a back burner. "I'm afraid the degree got lost in the shuffle," she said. "Although I have done a few layouts, a bit of design and copy writing over the years for different companies in Little Rock—when time would allow."

He grinned. "So I hear."

"You and my mother must have had a *long* talk."

"So we did. Would you like to see the furniture now?"

"If it isn't inconvenient."

"A sale is never inconvenient," he assured her. "We'll walk over to the Outlet and have a look."

It was obvious how Reed had come by his charm. Lately, Reed had entered her thoughts often. She'd been in town two days and had seen no sign of him. Abby was unsure whether she *wanted* to see him and yet...

"How *is* Reed?" she finally asked.

"Good." Ben was rubbing his chin thoughtfully. "At least, I think he's okay these days. You know, he'll be happy you're back. He always did have a special... well, hell, you know he was crazy about you."

Abby wasn't at all convinced of that. "For a time we were great friends, the three of us," she said more to herself than Ben. In school they'd been thrown together because of the alphabetical seating arrangement teachers had insisted on.

Out of school, though, Abby wasn't certain what had brought them together and kept them that way for years, before things had...changed.

"You know," Ben said, "I always held on to the idea that you'd be the one to give my son a well-deserved swift kick, marry him and somehow turn him around in the right direction, not necessarily in that order. But then you fell for Jason and... Crazy, huh, the way things happen."

Yeah, crazy, she thought with a silent sigh. She couldn't honestly say the same scenario had not crossed her mind off and on over the years. But somehow she doubted the wisdom in trying to make Reed Mackintosh do anything he didn't want to do.

"I don't believe I ever had much influence on Reed. Mostly he thought I was a real pest," she admitted. "But I'd be willing to bet that once he made up his mind, he managed to turn himself around. Quite nicely, from what I hear."

"Sure he has. After several crazy relationships—I guess that's what they're calling affairs these days—and a brush or two with the law, and any number of disappearing acts, when I didn't hear from him for months at a time. But hey, who's counting?"

Abby pressed on gently. "But he's finally come home and joined you in the business, hasn't he? Isn't that what you always wanted? I wasn't in town for half an hour before I heard he'll be taking over the company when you retire. I don't think he'd be ready to do that if he hadn't changed at least a little."

Ben groaned his concession. "When it comes to the business, yes, he's come a long way. When it comes to life, good sense and giving an old man some grandkids, well..." Ben shrugged as if further explanation was unnecessary.

"Still, you must be rather proud of him," Abby coaxed.

"Mmm," Ben murmured absently and tossed his pencil to the desk. "Anyway, it's nice to see that you're still defending him after all these years."

"Why wouldn't I? Jason always said—"

"Jason." Ben nodded thoughtfully. "Now, there's the biggest success story ever to come out of this town. From the day he was born, that kid knew what he wanted and went after it. He let nothing and no one stop him. That's what set him apart from everybody else, including Reed," he added.

Right, Abby thought. Jason had never let anyone, including her, get in the way of what he wanted. That's why the cancer had been such an unbelievable, unacceptable diagnosis. Because that kind of thing just didn't happen to people like him—people who were in control. Of themselves. The world. Everything.

Ben cleared his throat. "I know I told you this at the funeral," he said. "But you must know how sorry I am that... you know, that things have turned out this way. It's a damn shame, that boy dying. And so young. That last year must have been hell for you, watching him slip away. If there's anything I can do, anything you need, just ask and it's yours."

Abby swallowed hard and got up to leave. "Thank you, Mr. Mackintosh. People like you have been wonderful to me and my children."

"Around here, everybody was crazy about you and Jason. I have to admit, I was so proud of that boy, sometimes it was like he was my own son."

"Too bad he wasn't," Reed said easily—perhaps a little too easily—from the doorway. "I'm sure Jason never gave his pop half the trouble I gave you."

"You got that right," Ben said. "But how else would I have learned the name of every teacher, principal and truant officer in the school system...not to mention every cop in the county?"

Reed smiled at the floor, conceding his father's point, even though Abby knew it was a flagrant exaggeration of Reed's adolescent woes.

And then he turned his attention to her and she got the full effect of his craggy, dark good looks. A reminiscent ache—old and bittersweet—curled inside her. Abby was powerless to vanquish the feeling. But she was damned if she would reveal it. Not to Reed Mackintosh...or anyone else.

"Hello, Abby. It's been a long time."

An understatement if she'd ever heard one. "Yes, it has. How have you been?"

Reed gave her a brief embrace. Abby didn't dare let herself enjoy it. She wasn't sure if he actually said the obligatory "fine" in answer to her question. Gone was the hint of amusement she had noted before. Now she saw uncertainty in green eyes that were giving her face a thorough going over. She began to wonder if her mascara had smudged. Or maybe she was blushing.

Abby stepped away and realized he'd been holding her hand. When he let go, the sudden loss of warmth left her feeling a little empty. "It's good to see you again," she said, not nearly so easily as she would have liked. But Abby meant it sincerely. "You're looking very well." She meant that, too. Reed had not lost one bit of the good looks he had inherited from his father. His hair was a trifle longer than she usually liked, but it suited him.

"As a matter of fact, before you came in," Ben said to Reed, "we were also talking about you. About how well you've come around since...those days."

"Cussed and discussed it, have you?" Reed asked.

Abby realized she was in the middle of something here that she didn't quite understand. On the surface, it looked like any good-natured teasing between a father and son, but she didn't believe she was imagining the tension threading through the casual tone both men had taken.

"Abby's here to see Everlasting," Ben said.

Reed's green eyes squinted in her direction. He opened his mouth to say something and then apparently decided against it.

"Wrong choice?" Abby asked. She couldn't decide if he was pleased or not.

"Not at all. I wasn't aware that your tastes ran toward traditional, that's all." Now he did seem pleased. "For that matter, I wasn't even aware that you were coming home." He look pointedly at Ben. "No one saw fit to tell me."

His father shrugged. "What am I, the town crier? Look, Abby, I've gotta run now. I'll let Reed here show you the furniture—you don't mind, do you? I'll come by your mother's later to make delivery arrangements if you decide that's really what you want. Oh, and one more thing..."

"Yes?" Well aware that something—she hadn't a clue as to what—had changed, Abby could see that Ben Mackintosh now seemed in an awfully big hurry to get out of there.

"Before you even look at it, I want it understood that this furniture is on the house."

So that was it. "Mr. Mackintosh, I couldn't possibly let you do that. Really, I insist on paying for it."

"Absolutely not. I won't sell it to you."

"But why?"

"If you want the truth, I have a proposition for you that I'll tell you more about when you're settled in. Believe me, things'll go much better if you're at least a little beholden."

"Go better for whom?" she asked.

"Why, me, of course." He was obviously proud of himself. "And just to get things rolling in the right direction, don't you think it's time you called me Ben?"

Abby wasn't sure she could do that, but Reed held up a hand delaying any argument she might have made. He took her arm and motioned toward the door.

# Chapter Two

In a matter of moments they were alone.

She and Reed.

Somehow Abby hadn't expected that to happen. Now that it had, a couple of blinks seemed in order. Maybe a deep breath or two.

Abby didn't do either. She stood in the hallway reviewing the situation, fully aware of his palm warming the small of her back. "You know, if you're busy, Reed, I can wait. I mean, I could come back some other time."

So, she could wait, he thought. The trouble was that Reed didn't think *he* could. He wanted time, a lot of time, to look at her, take in the creaminess of her skin, the deep blue of her eyes, the slight upturn of her nose. She was behaving as if the two of them hadn't parted on a devastatingly final note years before. Or maybe it had only been devastating for him. There was a question in the lift of her brows. And he realized she was waiting for him to respond.

"No need to wait," he said, coaxing Abby slowly down the hallway to the outside. "You know, we do have a few pieces of Everlasting in the Sample Shop. It's a lot closer if you'd rather—"

"No, no, the Outlet will do fine," she said, knowing that the Sample Shop would not be a good idea.

Too private. Much too private on a Saturday morning with everyone gone for the weekend. Reed might want to talk about Jason. She needed to be out in the fresh air today, with people. As many people as possible. It was part of the new regimen she had lately prescribed for herself.

"It's a beautiful day," she said, "and I don't mind the walk at all."

Abby felt a little more confident once they were out of the building and in the sunshine again. Her mind relaxed, and she gave in to a memory of another Saturday morning long ago. In the Sample Shop.

She had received, or rather administered, her very first real kiss in that big barn of a building. Reed had been the recipient. As she recalled, the action had had a rather unsettling effect on him. And her.

Even now, the memory of her teenage brazenness caused her cheeks to flame—that and the memory of being caught by Mr. Hemphill, the security guard. Abby would always love that old man for turning his back and pretending not to notice her and Reed awkwardly wrapped around each other like two electrically-charged octopuses.

"You're looking wonderful," Reed said quietly as they walked past Glover's Antiques. "Have I already told you that?"

Abby couldn't remember. In any case, she didn't mind hearing it again. In fact she felt the smallest thrill and searched for something to say that would return the compliment.

Somehow, "I love the way you're filling out your jeans these days" didn't seem quite right. But the truth was that his jeans and the lightweight sport jacket he was wearing over a navy blue T-shirt supported her opinion that Reed had always kept himself in fine shape with very little bother doing so.

"Are you staying with your folks?" he asked.

"Only for a few more days. Until the rest of our things arrive and some of the repairs are done on the house. I don't think Mother and Dad could stand us much longer than that."

"I'm sure they're glad to have you. All of you. But I can see why you'd want to get settled in your own place soon. Tell me about Matthew and . . . Molly, isn't it?"

"Yes. Molly. She's five and never stops chattering. And then there's her brother, who's fourteen and has nothing to say at all anymore."

Reed nodded understanding. "It's a tough age to be."

"So I hear," she said noncommittally.

"Give him time. It'll work out."

"I suppose," she said, also in the same tone.

He wasn't touching her as they moved along together, but she could feel the warmth emanating from him, especially when he stopped and pulled her close to allow two boys on bicycles to pass them on the sidewalk. As soon as the path was clear again, she tried to step away, but Reed hesitated, still holding her arm.

Abby wasn't certain why the action alarmed her. But it did. It was a small, perfectly harmless gesture from someone she had known all her life. And yet she couldn't remember the last time any man had looked at her with such . . . thoroughness.

"Abby," he said raggedly, looking down at her, "I can't tell you how much—" He took in a breath and let it out again. "You know, I came to visit once . . . toward the end. You and the kids were out, but—"

"I know. Jason told me."

"I made my peace with him, Abby."

She knew that, too. "Look, Reed, it's all right. It hardly matters anymore."

"It matters to me," he said. "It matters a lot to me. I need to know how you feel about... things. Have you forgiven me for... hitting him?"

"Of course I've forgiven you. Although I've never understood what really happened that night or why the two of you fought—"

"Hey, you two, wait up!"

Even though she welcomed Rebecca Wayne's friendly interruption, Abby couldn't look away from the masculine green eyes that still held her. His dark brows had drawn together in an expression that she simply couldn't read. It was apparent that he wasn't going to offer any explanation for his behavior that night. Neither had Jason. Not one she could believe anyway. But that was all right. She wasn't certain she wanted to know anymore.

"Like I said, it hardly matters now."

"Abby, I'm sorry," he said. "I'm sorry I wasn't there to—"

"Reed, please don't," she pleaded. Abby could feel her nerves starting to unravel. He was the one person whose sympathy, whose own pain, would be her undoing.

"Hey, there!" Rebecca said.

Reed glanced away impatiently. Abby felt his hold on her arm relax. "All right, I won't. But I do want you to know I'm glad you've come home," he said finally and then let go of her altogether. "Hello, Becky."

Adjusting the sleeve of a color-splashed, off-the-shoulder peasant dress still sporting the dangling price tag, a barefoot Rebecca quickly tiptoed along the hot sidewalk to the shady spot where Abby stood with Reed.

"Morning, Reed, Abby," she said a little breathlessly.

"Hi, Becky." Abby looked at her watch. "It can't be noon already."

"No, no," Becky said, pushing back a thick strand of the naturally curly red hair that Abby had envied as far back as kindergarten. "I still have a few errands—like paying for this dress—but I thought, since you're downtown already, I could pick you up in front of the courthouse instead of at your mother's.''

"Don't tell me," Reed said to Becky. "You also knew Abby was coming home."

"Of course I did. Didn't you?" Becky turned a teasing shoulder to Reed's resigned expression, reminding Abby that some things—and some people—never changed. Anyway, not Becky, who had been flirting shamelessly and getting away with it for as long as Abby could remember. "We're going over to the Red Rooster for lunch and some long overdue girl talk."

"Hmm, the Red Rooster," Reed said. "That new place over in Fayetteville? The one with the so-called singles bar?"

"That's the one," Becky said with a singsong taunt.

"I see. Does my friend, Tom, know about this?" To Abby's delight, Reed began to return the teasing. "I mean, you *are* going to a place known to be frequented by frustrated males, young and old alike, looking for—God only knows what they're looking for—while poor Tom is slaving away at the Bed and Breakfast. A business that you dragged him into, kicking and screaming all the way," he added for Abby's greater understanding. "Poor Tom knows about this?"

"Yes, poor Tom knows about this," Becky said. "Not the frustrated men, of course," she noted quietly, with a small smile.

"Tsk, tsk," Reed chided so soberly that Abby had to smile. "One afternoon with you and the whole town'll be talking about her before sundown."

"Well, one can only hope." It was Becky again, relentless to the end. "Your problem is that you want to go, too, don't you? Well, don't even think about it. This is an impromptu class reunion of sorts. We're going to meet a few other women who Abby hasn't seen in years and talk over old times."

Reed studied the pavement. Abby had a feeling wild horses couldn't have dragged him to the Red Rooster today with Rebecca Wayne and company. Still, he held on like a dog with a bone, slipping Abby a wink before he faced his worthy opponent once more.

"Sure you wouldn't like me to come along? I mean, how can you have an authentic school reunion without at least one man?" he asked. "I don't mind representing the whole class. I could be the...token frustrated male, the designated hitter, whatever you want to—"

"Oh, no, you don't," Becky said. "I didn't say our reunion had to be 'authentic.' And we'll find our own frustrated male, if you don't mind. Besides, you'll just hustle all the single women."

"Who says they have to be single?" he challenged, chucking her chin. "And who says Abby and I don't have our own old times to talk over?"

"Yeah? Well, then make your own date with her," Becky returned spiritedly.

Reed appeared to be thinking it over before he spoke again. "All right, I will." He turned his back on Becky, effectively cutting her out of Abby's view as well as the conversation. "What do you say, Abby? Ditch Becky and have lunch with me."

"What do you mean 'ditch Becky'?" Unable to let the playful snub pass, Becky elbowed her way around him on the sidewalk. Abby could only shake her head at the two of them and their nonsense. But the truth was that she felt exhilarated by all the sparring for her company—particularly Reed's side of it—teasing or not.

"Tell him you're busy, Abby. He deserves it," Becky said.

"Why, that would be downright cruel," Reed announced, "especially to a man with my particular... sensibilities."

"Ha!" Becky faced him again. "Please, Reed, we *know* you, remember? So don't ask us to fall for that line."

"Why, I don't believe I was asking you," Reed said smoothly, before he took Abby's hand in his and pressed it to his lips.

He looked every inch the ardent lover, darkly handsome, snapping green eyes staring down at her. His hair, brushed back from his face, emphasized the lean square of his jaw. A shadow of a day's growth of beard darkened an already tanned complexion.

His mouth was soft and warm against her skin, and Abby had to remind herself sternly that this was, after all, a joke. That she had grown up with Reed Mackintosh and had watched him turn into one of the most charming, insincere, sensual flirts known to man—but with *other* women. Not with her. She herself had never been the target of his charm, his insincerity or his sensuality.

Only his friendship. And even that had been guarded at times. Abby also had to remind herself that passersby had begun to stop and stare, some of them small children.

"I'm waiting, Abby. If not today, then what about to-morrow evening?"

"Oh, for God's sake, put him out of his misery," Becky said.

"Yes, Abby, put me out of my misery," he cajoled.

Before Abby could respond, Becky jumped in again. "She's having dinner with me and Tom next Friday, Reed. If you'd like to come, too, we'd be happy to have you. There. How's that?" Becky said and sighed her impatience as if she couldn't understand why two mature adults couldn't work these things out for themselves.

"Why, thank you, Becky," Reed said without looking away from Abby. "Would that be all right with you, Abby? Will you have dinner with me—and Tom and Becky, of course—on Friday?" he asked and gave her a smile she was certain would sway any and every woman who ever made the mistake of taking him seriously.

But she wasn't about to make that mistake. Abby snatched her hand from his.

"Don't be silly, Reed. We're old friends, remember? I have no objection to your coming to dinner. And since when did you ever ask my permission to do *anything?*"

"Then I guess it's all settled." Just like that, his tone had become distant, but still pleasant, though, as if he hadn't quite gotten what he wanted, but was willing to make the best of it. Abby could only wonder what more he had wanted from her.

"Well, I've got to get back to Belle's before she thinks I've stolen this dress," Becky said. "By the way, what do you think of it?"

"It's beautiful," Abby offered, but she could see that Becky was more interested in the male point of view.

"It's definitely you," Reed said, nodding agreeably. "And I wouldn't give a second's thought to the five or six pounds it adds to your hips. On you . . . it looks fine."

"Oh, really," Becky murmured. "Thank you so much, Reed, for that honest if risky opinion. See you at noon," she said to Abby. "And Reed, I can't tell you how happy I am that next Friday you'll be at my culinary mercy."

Despite the confident smile Becky gave him, Abby knew the dress's fate was sealed. Doomed to at least one more day on the rack at Belle's.

As she and Reed continued on to the Outlet, Abby realized that during the past few minutes she had probably reached a milestone in her life since Jason's death. No, since *before* Jason's death. Someone had just involved her, Abby Malone, the widow, in a light, meaningless, *fun* conversation, one that hadn't weighed her down with memories, or sorrow, or sympathy. Abby had begun to wonder if such a thing would ever happen again.

How refreshing that it had!

"Thank you," she said without looking at the man walking beside her.

"You're welcome," he said easily. "Care to tell me the reason for your thanks?"

"Maybe. Someday."

"That's all right. I'm a patient man."

"Since when?"

"Let's just say it's a recent development."

"Oh. Care to tell me the reason for it?"

"Maybe." He opened the door to the Outlet and swept her into the cool interior. "Someday."

The sweet scent of lilac whispered around the great room. Abby smelled it as soon as she opened the window, letting in a rain-soaked breeze, cool for August, even in Winston.

Her and Jason's things would soon be in a whole different world, she thought, taking a deep breath of the Rollins place. High ceilings. Beautiful moldings. Refinished hardwood floors. Everywhere she looked there was new paint, new plaster. All for her. Her and Matthew and Molly.

Abby wasn't certain why she had felt such a strong need to get over here today, but after brunch with Jason's parents, she had asked them to drop her and the children off for another look around. Even though the furniture wouldn't arrive until the next day, she was already beginning to think of the place as home.

A good place to put her family back in order, she thought, turning to the wide bay window again. A black wrought-iron fence framed the yard in a nineteenth-century setting. Abby liked it. She thought she was going to like it a lot more. The wraparound wood porch. Sturdy white columns. Slate blue shutters. The house was nothing like the one she had left in Little Rock with its hard geometric lines and contemporary earth tones, much more to Jason's taste than to hers.

She stepped over the rolled-up Oriental rug in the entry on her way to the open front door where she could hear Molly outside calling to her brother.

"Whadda ya want?" Matthew demanded.

Abby could barely hear the small voice coming from somewhere in the side yard. "I told you I'm stuck. I need help."

"Well, help yourself," Matthew returned grumpily. "I'm busy."

Abby walked onto the porch so that her son could see his mother very clearly. When she crossed her arms and fixed him with a warning look, Matthew stopped swinging his stick and sighed, squinting into the bright sunlight.

"Mom, she's gone and got herself stuck in the stupid tree. If she's big enough to get up there, she oughtta be able to get herself down."

Abby continued to stare until finally he tossed the stick aside and slouched his way toward his sister. "Jeez, Molly, you're such a baby. When I was your age I climbed trees ten times higher than this, and nobody had to help me get down."

Abby sat on the steps and smiled, wondering where she had been when all this terribly impressive climbing had been going on.

"This tree's nothing but a weenie," Matthew continued his carping. "There. Now, don't bother me anymore."

"It is not a weenie," Molly defended herself, wiping her hands on her new Sunday outfit as she rounded the corner of the house. "Mama says it's a redbud. Isn't it a redbud, Mom?"

"Yes, I believe it is indeed a redbud," Abby said, eyeing the length of white lace now dangling from the hem of Molly's petticoat.

"See there?" Molly skipped up the steps and promptly sat beside her mother. "It is a redbud."

"Aw, who cares," Matthew said, jamming his hands into the pockets of his dark slacks. "It's still a weenie, and so are you."

Molly's mouth dropped open and promptly shut tight again.

"That's enough, Matthew." Abby pulled her daughter closer for a gentle tidying of hair the same shade as her own.

The same shade as Matthew's, too, Abby noted. Both her children had inherited her dark hair and blue eyes, a sharp contrast to Jason's fair skin and sandy blond all-American look. But it appeared that Matthew was going to be as tall as his father had been, if not quite as muscular. One could never tell, though, since boys had a way of changing so much in the last few growth years.

Abby did what she could to straighten her daughter's clothing and then sent her inside to look for Jemima, the temporarily lost cloth doll that Molly counted as her best friend.

"We'll be walking over to Grandmother's soon," Abby said with a parting pat to Molly's seat before she looked up to see Matthew still staring at her. "What is it, son?"

"Why do you always have to take her side?" he demanded testily, although Abby failed to see how she had taken anyone's side. "And why'd ya have to bring us to this stupid town to live in this stupid house with all these stupid people?"

Here we go again, she thought. "I did it for us," Abby said, hoping her son would follow her example and lower his voice a decibel or two. "For all of us, Matthew. You have two sets of grandparents here, and they'd like the chance to get to know their grandchildren."

"So? We didn't have to move here for that, Mom. We could've just visited more. There's *nothing* to do here. You *know* that. I hate this place."

"When school starts in a few weeks—"

"Oh, right. School. Have you *seen* that dump?"

"Yes, I have. I graduated from that school, remember? And with the new gym and other renovations, one could hardly call it a dump."

But her son was in no mood to listen, she noticed. Her son was in a mood to harangue. About life. His life in particular.

"Matthew, when you get to know the town and make some friends—"

"I don't want any friends here. I had friends in Little Rock. But do you care? No! Do you care about me at all? No! Dad would have listened. But do you listen? No!"

"Son, I know you're unhappy right now, but—"

"Yeah, I'm unhappy. And it's all your fault."

Abby could feel herself getting angry—again. She knew he was simply pushing her buttons. Still, the words hurt. He had been rude that morning and rude the day before. To most everyone he'd come in contact with. And lately his lip had a way of curling that annoyed her no end.

Abby stood and brushed the dust from her skirt. "Why don't we go into the house, Matthew?"

"I don't want to go in the house. I told you I hate this house. Dad would never have made us come here."

"We've been over this a dozen times," she said, aware that Matthew really had no idea what his father would or would not have done. "I made the decision I thought was right for us. And if your father were here, I think he would agree that this—"

"Oh, sure, blame Dad for everything," Matthew said, glaring at her resentfully.

"I'm not blaming your father."

"Then what gives you the right—"

"I'm your mother," she said evenly. "That gives me the right, and I will do what *I* think is best."

"Even when it's not fair?"

"Even when it's not fair."

"Well, that's just plain stupid," he said, "and if you think I'm gonna like it here, then you're just as stu—"

Her brow was arched and waiting for him to finish the word that would cinch his fate for the afternoon. Abby stood her ground even though her son was at least two inches taller than she. Even though he was fairly bursting with anger. And hurt. But Abby couldn't think of a thing to do about it.

Matthew didn't say any more. For months he'd been rejecting her or anyone else's attempts at affection or comfort. The bitterness in his eyes made it clear that he planned to continue in that vein. Maybe she *was* wrong. Maybe she *had* made a mistake, bringing the children here.

Then all at once, her son shrugged defeat and turned away. Although he appeared to be giving up this particular battle, Abby knew from experience that the war wasn't over by any means. "Where are you going?" she asked.

His answer was a resounding slam of the gate as he left the yard. Abby considered calling him back to demand better manners, but she swallowed the urge. Perhaps it was best if he had some time alone.

It was then that she noticed Reed.

# Chapter Three

He was standing on the sidewalk just outside the fence, and when Matthew passed, Reed stopped the boy with a well-timed greeting. "Afternoon. You're Matt Malone, aren't you?"

Abby's son muttered something she couldn't make out and he refused to look up. Still, Reed didn't appear to take offense. He simply held out a hand.

"I'm Reed Mackintosh. Your dad was a friend of mine. I thought a lot of him. Everyone around here did."

For what seemed like minutes, Abby waited for her son to make up his mind to shake Reed's hand. When he finally made the effort, halfhearted though it was, she let out the breath she'd been holding. Matthew was making an effort to respond. Abby hoped it was some sort of thanks for Reed's kind words. She hoped her son was showing that he could behave in a civilized fashion even when he didn't much feel like it.

"Well, I won't keep you," Reed said. "Just wanted to say hello and let you know we're glad to have you and your family here. Let me know if there's anything I can do to help you get settled."

"Uh . . . thanks," Matthew replied uncertainly, scratching the back of his head.

"While I'm here, I think I'll have a word with your mother," Reed said. "See you around town, Matt."

The tension in her neck subsided as her son continued slowly down the street. As she watched Reed unlatch the gate and come into the yard, she was grateful that he had been so friendly in spite of Matthew's aloofness.

"Hello, Reed. I didn't expect to see you until dinner at Becky's."

"Dad's having his usual afternoon nap, and I opted for a stroll." Making his way up the sidewalk, he gave each shirtsleeve a couple of turns, exposing tanned and muscular forearms. Although his khaki pants looked fresh enough, the odor of varnish or lacquer of some sort lingered around him. As far back as she could remember, furniture had been the one constant in Reed's life.

"Working on Sunday?" she asked. Sitting down, she motioned for him to join her.

He dropped down to the step and sat beside her. "Not really. There's a small personal project I've been trying to finish and—" He frowned a bit and Abby got the full effect of his attractive green eyes. "How could you tell?"

"It must be that scintillating cologne you're wearing."

He brought his shirtsleeve up for a whiff and then let out his breath. "Tung oil. I didn't realize it was so pungent."

"But not unpleasant." She meant that. Abby had always appreciated the scents of wood and woodworking. "Do you and your father still live in the house on Adelaide?"

"Dad does. A few years ago, I bought a house a couple of blocks over, next door to Miss Walsh and her sister, if you can believe that." Reed looked thoughtful. "Of course, it's a stupid place, too, as you might imagine. Almost as stupid as this one. But what can you expect when it's on a stupid street in a stupid town with so many stupid people?"

Abby's chin dropped. "How much did you hear?"

"Well, let's see. I counted at least ten more stupids, five or six you-don't-cares, a very impressive couple of weenies, and my personal favorite, it's-all-your-fault. How does that square with your tally?"

It was clear he had heard all that mattered. "I guess it could've been worse."

"A lot worse," he agreed. "I take it your son didn't want to make the move to Winston."

"He's still pretty angry about it. But then he's angry about most everything these days."

"Resistance and anger," Reed said. "Words to live by when you're fourteen. And oh, how they love to get indignant. It's age-typical."

Abby wondered what Reed, who had no children of his own, could possibly know about teenagers or "age-typical" behavior. "I hope he wasn't rude."

"To me?" Reed shook his head. "I'd say he was more suspicious than anything. Gave me a wary look. Not unlike the one his mother's giving me now."

She turned away from his sidelong glance. "Sorry. It's just that I've been dealing with this for some time now. I was hoping the move to Winston would help."

"Maybe it will. But give it time. You just got here."

He was right, she supposed. After all, Matthew was basically a decent human being, *human* perhaps being the operative word here.

"Hey, while I'm here, how about the ten-cent tour of your new digs?" Reed stood and reached for her hand to pull her up beside him. "You can show me where you want the new bedroom furniture. All right if we deliver it first thing in the morning?"

"Of course," she said, wondering if Reed was going to take personal charge of the job. "The master bedroom's upstairs at the end of the hall."

"What made you choose this place anyway?"

Abby led him into the entryway and past the curved staircase into the great room, empty except for a floor lamp and wing chair, both donated by her mother. "I guess I wanted to get away from what Jason and I had—I mean the kind of house we had—to something a little softer, warmer, with curves instead of so many angles, more traditional."

"Hey, my thoughts exactly."

She shook her head. "Well, I don't know about traditional, Reed. But your weakness for lots of soft and curvy is pretty well known. At least in these parts."

"Is that so?" His voice became quiet, his expression thoughtful. "You know, people in these parts might not know me as well as they think they do. That's not to say I don't like women, because I do...very much. But just because I haven't settled down with one...well, that doesn't mean..."

Reed shook himself free of whatever he had been about to say, and she realized that he didn't much appreciate comments about his personal life, especially the part women played in it.

"Well, anyway, about the house," he said. "You decided to go traditional."

"That's part of it." The house also seemed protective, but she didn't want to say that to Reed. "You remember the Rollins family. Eight kids all talking at once. I used to walk by here every day on my way to school and hear them. Every morning sounded like total chaos. It always seemed like so much fun. Such a...well, a loud, happy home." Abby winced inwardly at the sappy cliché.

"I see. And you're hoping some of that happiness might have rubbed off and stayed with the house?"

"I suppose it does sound a little silly, but I can't help wanting some good cheer...some loud, good times for my children. Not that my own childhood wasn't happy," she declared despite Reed's attempts to hold back a smile. "It's just that my upbringing was so orderly and quiet, so uncluttered, so...oh, I don't know...."

"Proper?"

"No," she said defensively. "At least, I didn't think of it in that way. It's just that my life seemed to sail on such an even keel all the time. Maybe it was because I was so—"

"Biddable?" he supplied.

It sounded so dull.

"My dad would have been ecstatic over *semi*biddable," Reed said. "The fact that you did everything you were told—"

"That's hardly a fair statement."

"Oh, no?" he teased. "Correct me if I'm wrong, but at graduation, didn't you get some sort of award for never missing a day of high school?"

Or elementary. Or junior high. But Abby saw no good reason to set the record even straighter.

"And as I recall, there were never any detentions to blacken the good name of Abigail Lindstrom."

"I had a healthy respect for authority. That's all."

"I'll say. Remember your sixteenth birthday party at the pool?" he pressed. "Weren't you the girl whose mother talked her out of wearing a bikini? A deep disappointment to the male guests, I can tell you. It wasn't your color, I believe she said. And then on the senior camp-out, when Jason got sick and couldn't make it, your dad wouldn't let you ride in my car to Kyle's Landing on the Buffalo."

"He didn't actually say I couldn't," she corrected.

"Right. 'Why, tarnation, ya never know when it might come a tornado,'" Reed said in a near-perfect imitation of her father. "'And think how worried poor ol' Jas'd be.'"

Abby smiled, wondering how Reed could possibly remember more about her past than she did.

"I could go on," he said. "There's college, too. Your dad chose the place. And your mother strongly suggested your major."

Even though she wouldn't have put things quite that way, Abby couldn't deny any of it. And so she said nothing.

Reed turned away to stare out the bay window. "Hell, you even married a guy who was father-tested and mother-approved," he said quietly. "Nobody else ever had a chance."

Had she imagined the hint of bitterness in his voice? "You're right," she agreed. "My family loved Jason."

A long moment passed before Reed faced her again. "So did I. But that isn't the point. You never even dated anyone else."

No, she hadn't. But if she had... Abby had often wondered. Would her life have been different? Jason had always been so sure of her.

Abby looked at Reed. "You've got a point. Most of the time, I've avoided conflict in my life."

"Every time, I'd say."

No, Abby thought. Not every time. Admittedly the adolescent differences with her parents had been few. Reed would have been surprised to know that some of them had involved him. But she wasn't about to discuss any of these things with him. Neither was she ready to reveal the very adult conflict she'd had with Jason during their marriage. Conflict that had very nearly destroyed her.

"Face it, kid. You're just too damned agreeable," he said. "But it's hardly a character flaw. And I noticed you haven't passed that particular trait along to at least one of your offspring."

Which brought them back to Matthew. Oddly enough, safer ground to Abby's way of thinking.

"If I could just get my stubborn son off to a good start," she said. "And on the right track. What do young people do for entertainment in Winston these days?"

Reed didn't appear eager for such a quick change of subject. Still, after a moment, he moved from the window. "A lot of kids his age hang out at the Cue Center downtown."

"A pool hall?"

"Yes, and video games along with fast food. But it's more a family atmosphere than you might think. Even the younger kids are welcome. And an occasional adult is not unheard of."

"I see. You seem to know a lot about the place."

"Of course I do. I'm the occasional adult," he announced.

"Now that you mention it, I'd heard that about you."

"Heard what?"

She shrugged. "That you were an occasional adult."

"Oh," he said with a nod, "so you think you're a wise guy, huh?" He took one step toward her before he stopped himself. It was all he could do to keep from grabbing her and . . . well, he wasn't sure what he would have done to Abby. Held her? Kissed her? At the moment, just grabbing her would have been more than he had ever hoped for. But Reed didn't dare. He didn't suppose she was ready for that. Hell, he wasn't sure *he* was ready for that.

In any case, she had already turned away in thought, obviously on a different track than he was.

"You know," she said, "if you're right about this place, maybe tomorrow afternoon Molly and I could go with him. I know a little about pool, and—"

"Uh . . . why not let me introduce him to some guys his age who could show him around," Reed offered. "It'll give him a chance to . . . get his bearings. Be on his own a little."

Abby sighed. "Well, why not? I guess at this point it's best for a mother to stay out of sight as much as possible."

"Maybe. Just until he makes his own friends, gets to know the town. By the way, there's a place near the river where some of the boys like to ride. Does Matt have a mountain bike?"

"I don't think he's been on it in ages. I'm not even sure it's in working condition."

"If he's interested, there are several bike nuts around who could help him get it in shape. There's a good bicycle shop on Main Street, too."

"Sounds fine." All in all she was encouraged by Reed's suggestions. As Abby made silent plans to locate the bicycle in storage as soon as possible, she noticed her son making his way quietly past the doorway toward the stairs. "Matthew, will you come in here, please?"

An all-too-audible sigh emanated from the hallway as the squeak of his sneakers preceded him into the room.

"Reed's just been telling me about some activities you might be interested in," Abby said. When her son lifted a doubtful eyebrow in Reed's direction, she hurried on. "If you'd like to get your bike in shape, Reed says there's a good bike shop downtown. On Main—"

"Yeah, I saw it yesterday. Looks pretty lame to me."

"It's only a suggestion," she said.

"Forget it, Mom. There's nothin' to do in this hick town."

"Maybe you haven't been looking in the right places."

"There aren't any 'right' places. And there's only one movie, Mom. One crummy theater."

"Matthew, you're being ru—"

"So you like movies," Reed interrupted. "I'll introduce you to Alan Whiteside. He runs the rec center at the park. Once a week he loads a van with kids and takes them over to Clarksville. It isn't that far, and there's a mall there and several theaters. Think you might be interested?"

"Naw, that's okay. I don't like movies that much anyway."

"Right," Reed said with a knowing nod. "Well, if you change your mind, Alan's at the rec center most mornings."

"Thank you for telling us about it," Abby returned, then looked pointedly at Matthew.

"Yeah. Thanks," he muttered unenthusiastically, and Abby wanted to shake him.

"You know, Matthew," she said. "Reed and your father and I grew up together here in Winston." *And I expect you to treat my friends with respect,* she added silently.

Matthew's only response was to cross his arms over his chest as he continued looking down at his shoes.

"He and your father were best friends," she persisted. "They found lots of things to do."

The boy shifted his weight to one foot and shrugged. "You play football, too?"

Reed smiled a little. "No, Matt, I didn't. Your dad was the football hero around here. Brought back the state championship three years in a row."

"So, what'd *you* do?"

"Ran track, mainly. Boxed a little."

"Boxing?" Matthew's head came up in the slightest degree of interest.

*At last,* Abby thought, a little surprised that the subject of Jason's high school football career hadn't received a better response, even though it was old news he had heard a thousand times. He appeared to be assessing Reed's physique, as though he might be doubting the man's sparring ability. Which had been considerable, she remembered, much as she had hated the sport.

"What division?" Matthew asked.

"Welterweight," Reed said.

"Ever win any titles?"

Again Reed smiled and shook his head. "No, I can't say that I did. Can't remember even coming close."

"Reed, that's not true," Abby said. "You did very well. Especially our senior year. I remember the coach saying that you had the Golden Gloves in the bag that sea—"

Then she remembered. Reed *had* had the championship sewn up that season, the Midsouth Golden Gloves in Jackson, Tennessee, sponsored by the *Memphis Commercial Appeal*. Weeks before the tournament, she had hyped the event and Reed's chances of winning in the school newspaper. Despite her doubts about the sport, Abby had ardently wanted him to win. Some positive recognition might have offset many of the negatives Reed had racked up for himself over the years. And he had come so close.

"Well, what happened?" Matthew asked, obviously trying to appear as indifferent as possible. "I mean, why *didn't* you win?"

"Complications," Reed said simply.

"Yeah? Like what?" Matthew was pressing the issue. Abby had to wonder why he chose this particular time to be nosy. "What kind of complications?"

"Matthew—" she said.

"It's all right, Abby," Reed cut in. "It was a million years ago. Besides, if I don't tell him, you can bet somebody else will. Hell, my own father still tells anyone who'll listen."

Abby looked at her son, who clearly had no intention of sparing Reed a full explanation.

"You see, Matt, I was lucky enough to make it to the finals," Reed said, "but on the last day of the competition, I never made it to the championship match. When I should have been in the ring, I was driving back to Winston. On the team bus. Without the team."

Matthew's eyes widened, unmasking clear interest before he dropped his gaze again. "You mean you came back alone?"

Reed said nothing.

"Why?" Matthew asked. "Did somebody die or somethin'?"

"No, but I came close when my dad found out what I'd done."

"You just took off with the bus? And didn't even tell anybody? Why?"

"Stupidity," Reed said. "That's all it was. I decided it would be more fun to steal the bus and beat the team home than to win the championship."

Matthew looked blankly at Reed for a moment and then shrugged his contempt. "Well, that was lame."

The soul of tact, Abby thought dryly. But it *was* lame. It sounded every bit as lame now as it had all those years before. As student manager of the team, Jason had gone to Jackson, too, but even he had never understood why Reed had pulled such a boneheaded stunt. But that was Reed's adolescence. Crazy.

Looking back now, Abby realized that every time Reed Mackintosh had come anywhere near success, he had shot himself in the foot. And even crazier was the fact that it had never seemed to matter to him.

"Matthew," she said, "run upstairs and find your sister. We should be getting to your grandparents soon."

When her son had left the room, Abby looked at Reed again. "You'll have to excuse him. He hasn't come very far in the sensitivity department."

"No need to apologize for him," Reed said. "The boy's right. It was irresponsible and, well, lame. But it hardly matters now."

She wondered. He had changed, certainly. Grown up and settled down, though not in the traditional way of marriage and family. According to Becky, he had established himself as a positive part of the community. But Abby could remember a time when all Reed had wanted was to get away from Winston. From life. From himself.

"Look, I can see you've got things to do," he said. "So I'll go now and—"

"But you haven't met Molly yet."

"How about in the morning when we bring the furniture?"

"All right. You'll like her," Abby said. "She isn't nearly as...as..."

"Challenging?"

"Well, at least not in the way Matthew is."

"Biddable, is she?"

His mouth curved, and Abby realized that from the moment Reed had opened the gate, she'd been waiting for just that look. Just that smile. "See for yourself in the morning," she said.

"I'll look forward to it," he promised.

When Reed had gone, Abby went to the window and closed it. He was simply an old friend, she cautioned herself. *Reassured* herself. But she realized with some alarm that she was feeling a little too cozy, a little too charmed, perhaps, for her own good.

# Chapter Four

Reed stopped by every day and a couple of evenings that week. And although he never stayed long, Abby noticed that his time was well spent, and he never arrived empty-handed. On Monday he delivered the promised furniture and then helped Matthew put together all the beds in the house. She appreciated his thoughtfulness in bringing any number of items he "just happened to remember" essential to setting up her new household. Light bulbs, kitchen matches, even fuses and various cleaning products, which had somehow escaped her shopping list.

On Wednesday he showed up with lunch and a teenage boy, who was put to work with Matthew erecting Molly's backyard swing set. Despite her initial protests, Abby came to look forward to Reed's daily visits. Molly adored him, she noticed, mostly because he knew all the words to "Sweet Molly Malone" and sang the song at every opportunity. By Thursday even Matthew hardly scowled each time he was asked to help out.

On Friday at sundown, Abby felt quite at ease walking with Reed to The Thomas Wayne Bed and Breakfast. Appearing none the worse for wear—in fact, looking quite spiffy in a casual shirt and slacks—she realized that he had managed to turn a grueling week's work into a thoroughly enjoyable experience. Now that the house was in some semblance of order, she viewed dinner with the Waynes as a well-deserved reward for both her and Reed's labors.

The feeling stayed with her through the glasses of wine they shared with Becky and Tom on the veranda before the four of them went upstairs to the Waynes' private quarters.

Even when Tom's sister, Katherine, swept into the dining room, said her hellos and immediately launched into her own personal tribute to Jason, Abby maintained her good humor. But half an hour later, when all attempts to change the subject had failed and Katherine was still going on about Jason, Abby began to feel the cheer slowly seeping out of her mood.

"Is it painful, dear?" Katherine put down her fork to lean closer. "I mean, does it bother you much to talk about him?"

Now she asks, Abby thought. It didn't bother her in the way that Katherine obviously meant. No one knew that, of course. Still, Abby—and she suspected everyone else—would have preferred another subject. "No, I wouldn't say it bothers me, but—"

"Good." Katherine reached over to pat Abby's hand. "Because I firmly believe it's wise to talk about these things. When my Edward died, I found that sharing my memories with others worked wonders. And now that Jason . . . well, you know how the whole town felt about him. He was simply the best," Katherine said. "There will never be another man like him."

"Thank you," Abby said.

"Tom," Katherine said, "do you remember that time on the Buffalo when our canoe wrapped around that tree and Jason had to latch onto a log and..."

Abby laid her napkin aside and looked across the table at Reed, who returned a reassuring wink. Throughout dinner, she'd been aware of his watchful eye as if he'd been trying to gauge any ill effects she might be suffering from all the reminiscing. Abby appreciated that, but he needn't have worried. She understood how people had loved her husband. She also understood their need to look back and remember. But so few of them seemed to understand her need to look ahead. To get on with life. She wasn't certain Reed understood it, either, but at least he didn't push.

"...Jason carried me all the way to the shore and then went back for my hat," Katherine said, touching her napkin to each corner of her mouth. "Abby, he was so generous. I don't think anyone in Winston will ever forget how much he gave to others."

"Thank you," Abby said again.

"Katherine, what about you?" Reed asked. "Anything new in Jonesboro?"

"Same old thing, really. Of course, it hasn't been easy running the hardware business alone now that Edward is gone, but—" she put a hand on Abby's shoulder "—we do the best we can, don't we?"

"It isn't as if you don't have help," Becky said casually. "Isn't Ron Glidewell taking care of the store while you're visiting us?" When Katherine smiled primly in response, Becky looked at Abby. "You know, for the longest time we've been hearing rumors that Ron would like to be more than her assistant manager."

The slightest blush crept into Katherine's cheeks. "Well, yes, Ronald *has* been after me to set a wedding date, but I'm not sure it's the right thing to do. It seems so disloyal...to Edward, I mean."

"Katy, it's been five years," Tom reminded his sister.

"I know," she said, "but that's the way it is when you've *really* loved a man and lived with him and know everything about him and...well, you just never get over the loss. Isn't that right, Abby?"

"Of course you get over it," Becky snapped. "At least anyone with half a br—" Looking up in time to notice her husband's wince, Becky smiled and lowered her voice. "The point is, people do eventually come to grips with the death of a spouse, Katherine. At least, most people do. After a while they take their families and their memories...and simply move on." Becky passed the basket of bread to Tom. "Wouldn't you want me to find someone else if anything happened to you?"

"Well, I wouldn't want you to get engaged at my wake, but...no, I wouldn't want you to be alone," Tom said. "I know *I'd* find someone. Could you pass the squash, please?"

His wife stared. "You would? But...you've always said I was one of a kind. That you could never—"

"Oh. Well, of course you are. That's why the search would be long and hard and...fruitless—no doubt about it—but as you say, one does have to move on."

None of this encouraged Becky to let go of the dish of fried squash she was holding, and Abby could feel Reed's amusement as Tom pressed on, keeping a covetous eye and a beefy hand on the dish.

"You know, sweetheart, now that I've had a chance to think about it...I'd have to join a monastery. That's all there is to it. How could I ever replace you?"

Another moment passed before Becky stopped frowning and gave up the squash. "Abby, would you help me with dessert? Katherine, we'll leave you to entertain the men, if that's all right."

"Of course," Katherine said easily.

Abby gathered several dishes from the table and left the room. By the time she reached the kitchen, Becky was already muttering to herself. "Entertain the men, ha. Sure to be a laugh a minute *there*."

Abby went to place the dishes in the sink.

"Out of the blue she shows up here first thing this morning," Becky said. "Just our luck we had an unoccupied room, and then, of course, Tom invited her to dinner with us. I could kick him for that."

Abby found herself laughing despite her friend's annoyance. "She's his sister, Becky. How could he *not* invite Katherine?"

"He could have made something up. That's how. We could have changed our plans and gone to a nice restaurant somewhere and—"

"And miss this fabulous dinner you made? Forget it." Abby dipped a finger into the homemade ice cream and tasted the frozen concoction. "Mmm. I can't wait to try this on your fresh peach cobbler. What can I do to help get this part of the show on the road?"

Becky pointed to a slotted spoon on the wall. "Dish up the cobbler. I'll take care of the ice cream. And why does she have to go on and on about Jason, for God's sake. Everybody knows growing up she had a thing for him. Everybody also knows he never gave her the time of day. But if she tells one more anecdote about your husband— Not that I had anything against the man, but honestly. What about *your* feelings? Of course, Katherine has always had the finesse of your average bull moose."

Abby smiled. "I don't mind. Really. Although I never realized there must be a million Jason Malone stories floating around this town. This past week I must have heard at least half of them, every time I went out of the house. So have Matthew and Molly, for that matter."

"And you like that?"

"In some ways it's good for my kids, I think. They've learned a lot about their father—some positive things that they didn't know before—even though Matthew sometimes seems to resent his father's popularity. But maybe hearing about Jason will allow them to somehow feel closer to him. Maybe closer than they—'' Abby stopped herself. It didn't seem right, what she'd been about to say.

"Closer than they actually were?" Becky finished knowingly.

Abby felt a certain relief. Despite the rekindling of a dear friendship with Becky, she wasn't sure that anyone in Winston, not even Becky Wayne, would understand.

"He was a doctor," Abby said, and wondered if she would ever stop defending his neglect. "A lot of people counted on him."

Becky nodded, but it was clear she wasn't buying that line. Not for a minute. Abby concentrated on filling the dessert bowls.

"Do you suppose that's part of the reason for your troubles with Matthew now?" Becky also kept her gaze on the job at hand.

"I don't know. It could be connected to his father, but I can't really say how much of it is grief and how much is love, or regret, or... just plain resentment."

"Or how much of it is just being fourteen," Becky reminded her. "You know, Reed does seem to have a way with teens. Maybe he can help."

"Oh, he already has. Or at least he's been trying. This past week he introduced Matthew to a young man who works at Charlie's. Frankie Benteen. Do you know him?"

Becky nodded. "He's had his problems, but basically he's a good kid. From a hardworking family of modest means, shall we say. I understand Reed has taken him in tow."

"Does he do that often? Take a special interest in a young person?"

"Yes, he does. And when you consider his background, who would know more about adolescent troubles than Reed Mackintosh?"

Abby couldn't disagree.

"You know," Becky said playfully, "word around town is that Reed's taken a special interest in a certain *adult* person, too. Someone he's been seen with every day since Saturday. Walking with her. Helping her get settled. Doing her shopping and making personal deliveries of furniture to her—that sort of thing. You wouldn't know anything about it, would you?"

Abby had to smile. She hadn't forgotten how quickly gossip, even the most innocent, could take hold and blossom in a place like Winston. "Does the town in all its wisdom know that these were simple acts of friendship? By an old friend?"

"The town has been duly informed of this," Becky reported dutifully.

"I take it the town still has doubts."

"I couldn't say. But said town has an awfully long memory of Jason and Abby sitting in a tree—that sort of thing," Becky said. "The town also has several memories of Reed, which he has not yet managed to overcome, mainly because he doesn't care to try."

Abby picked up the tray of desserts. "What are you getting at, Becky?"

Becky put an arm around Abby and hugged her close before letting her go again. "I'm simply saying that you're vulnerable right now, my friend. In more ways than you might be aware of. Just be patient. Don't . . . push things."

*Push things. What things?* Abby wondered on her way back to the dining room, where nothing much had changed in her absence. Reed and Tom were having a friendly discussion about some tax matter due to be addressed by the town council.

When she set Reed's dessert in front of him, he smiled his appreciation. "Looks larrupin' good, as Dad would say."

Abby could see nothing in his eyes—and she searched carefully—to alarm her or even make her cautious about him. There was friendship, of course, a certain long-standing affection, purely platonic as far as she could tell. How could there possibly be more when up until last Saturday she hadn't spoken to the man in years? The town was obviously full of . . . something. She wasn't sure what.

Even though she and Becky had been teasing, at times it had seemed to Abby that the town of Winston really did have a life of its own, assessing every move by its citizens, approving this one, disapproving that one, putting you so firmly in the place it wanted you that you couldn't get out if you tried.

Not that she herself had ever tried. Sometimes it seemed to her that all those years before, the town had paired her with Jason Malone before she'd even had a chance to think much about it. Maybe even before Jason had thought much about it. He, "the good guy," she "the good girl"—until later when her title was changed to simply "the good guy's girl." Likewise, Reed had been branded "the-reckless-and-a-little-bit-dangerous bad boy." Abby liked to think that she at least had changed, that she was stronger now and not so . . . biddable anymore.

She ate her cobbler and silently told the town to go to hell. Then she apologized, again silently, and said she didn't mean it. After all, Winston was once more going to be her home. And getting along was important, both for her and her children.

As Abby lifted the last spoonful to her lips, she noticed that Reed was staring. In fact, everyone in the room was staring. At her. "Sorry," she said, "I was thinking. Did I miss something?"

Reed got up and came around to her chair. "Becky suggested that you and I go downstairs for some air while she and Katherine make coffee. Tom has a couple of phone calls to return and then he'll join us. Shall we?"

"Yes," Abby said, "I'd like that."

Whether it was the wine or the gossip or a bit of both, Abby was feeling defiant. She didn't suppose anyone no-

ticed, though, since her rebellion had so far manifested itself only in her thoughts. But damn, Reed had been a good
friend to her, and there was no way she would forgo that
friendship simply to stop a few wagging tongues.

"Yes, I'd like that very much, Reed," she repeated and
went with him down the two flights of stairs to the porch.

Outside in the darkness, Abby moved to the corner rail-
ing and leaned a shoulder against the fluted column. Reed
followed and stood close beside her. The easy press of his
hands on her shoulders was warm and reassuring.

"Looks as if we've got ourselves another cool evening,"
he said. "And a crescent moon too. Wonder what we've
done to deserve such pleasant weather in the middle of August?"

Abby didn't know and so she said nothing.

"You got awfully quiet upstairs," he said. "Anything I
can do?"

"No, just . . . just be my friend, Reed."

At least she still considered him a friend, he thought.
"That's easy enough. Being your friend, I can honestly say,
is my pleasure."

"Thank you. That means a lot."

Reed closed his eyes and wondered if there was any way
in hell he could steal a pleasurable but friendly kiss. He
didn't want to rush, but hell, he'd been thinking about it all
evening. During the walk to the inn. Watching her sip the
glass of wine Tom had offered. The few times she had
smiled tolerantly at Katherine's more inane remarks. And
virtually *every* time he had witnessed her mouth closing
around a spoonful of ice cream. The coffee wouldn't brew
forever. He could imagine Becky crashing the porch at any
moment.

While he was weighing the possibilities, Reed felt Abby
stir beneath his touch. It was fast becoming a matter of now
or never. Ever so gently, he turned her to him. Slowly he
lifted her chin and, without checking the look in her eyes,

bent his head low to touch his lips to hers with excruciating restraint. It was a fine start, that feather-light kiss, but not nearly enough to make him let her go now.

So he kissed her again, this time daring to slide his hands a little farther around her waist and coax her a few degrees closer. When she didn't pull away, he began to wonder just what manner of paradise he had stepped into. Abby reached her arms around his neck, and for several seconds the soft pressure of her lips sapped all his strength the one moment, then the next, flooded him with heat like a slow evening tide. He rallied enough presence of mind to return both the kiss and the embrace before she could step back from him. But before he could fully savor the sweetness, her lower lip began to tremble—just enough to paralyze him—and then she broke the contact.

Reed allowed her to turn away from him, but he kept his arms ever so relaxed and casual around her waist. A sliver of moonlight cast the slightest glow on her hair, and Reed kept reminding himself to keep it light, keep it friendly, or it would all be over before it started, having only the vaguest idea what "it" was.

"Do you . . . know what you're doing?" he whispered.

"No," she whispered back. "I haven't a clue as to what I'm doing. Or why. So please don't . . . hold me responsible for— Maybe I was simply feeling thankful. In a . . . friendly sort of way."

She couldn't even admit an attraction to him. The thought annoyed him no end, but he answered. "Okay," he said, "I'll buy that."

"I suppose it was impulse. Caprice."

That was a little better, he decided. A little.

"I am not an impulsive person," she said. "Not normally."

"Well, I didn't *think* you were. . . ."

She gave him a patient over-the-shoulder stare.

"Okay," he said. "You're not impulsive."

"Thank you," she said simply, wondering if Reed believed any of her explanation. In fact, she couldn't recall doing anything so impetuous, so *un*-Abby since the last time she'd kissed Reed Mackintosh. And here she had gone and done it again. "Just don't...hold me to any of this. Please."

"Fine." Good Lord, he supposed he should be happy just holding her to *him*.

"It *is* a beautiful night, isn't it? I mean with the stars and everything."

"Absolutely." He answered quietly, fearing the contact would be broken by the slightest sudden move on his part. He was trying to be smart this time. Not like that day in the Sample Shop. This time she wouldn't bolt and run. This time he wouldn't let her. "Anything you say," he murmured.

"You're being awfully agreeable," Abby said.

Why wouldn't he be? He'd just kissed Abby Malone, and moments later he still had his arms around her. Still had her against his chest. Hell, he was positively brimming with agreeable and chock full of friendly. "Just my nature, I guess."

An easy chuckle emerged from Abby's lips and bubbled into a low throaty laugh so evocative that the wanting slowly oozed over his shoulders and all the way down to his groin. Reed thought she would surely sense the intensity and move away from him, but she didn't. When she rested her head against him and sighed, it was all he could do to keep from turning her around and kissing her again. Harder, more fully, on *his* terms this time. He steeled himself against such a move. Keep it casual, he cautioned himself again.

It had probably been awhile since she'd been kissed in any romantic way, he supposed. Maybe she simply wanted a good place to start. With someone she thought would be safe. If that was the case, she had definitely come to the wrong man. Because he wasn't safe by any stretch of the imagination. Not with Abby. Not if she was looking for practice without any feelings involved. Again, the possibility that she was the one taking advantage licked at his reason.

Then Abby went stiff in his arms. Her words came out breathy at first. "Why, hello, Miss Walsh. Henrietta. How nice to see the two of you."

Reed looked over to the sidewalk where Theodora Walsh's ramrod form could be seen even in the dim light emanating from the Wayne hallway. Henrietta, shorter and downright giddy in comparison, stood at her older sister's side.

"Good evening, Abigail," Henrietta said. "We heard that you and the children had come home."

"Yes," Abby said. "Just last week actually."

Miss Walsh stepped closer to the porch. "I'm sure your family is very pleased. As I imagine *you* are, Mr. Mackintosh."

In the shadows, Reed didn't know if the two elderly women could see his arms around Abby or what he should do about it if they could see. Abby answered the question for him. She was carefully nudging his arms away from her waist. He stepped aside and moved into the light. "I couldn't be happier," he admitted. "Are you ladies out for a stroll this evening?"

"Goodness, no," Henrietta said. "We've been at Genevieve Jenkins's house. This mornin' her daughter-in-law gave birth to her seventh child, you know. I swear someone should tell that girl what's causing—"

"Henrietta," Theodora said, "we really should be getting on home now."

"In a minute, Dori." The younger Miss Walsh looked up at the porch again. "Having a nice visit with the Waynes, are you?"

"Yes," Abby said. "Becky and Tom cooked a wonderful dinner for us."

"I see. Just the two of you?" Henrietta asked with a hint of suggestiveness.

"My children had previous plans," Abby explained. Reed could have sworn they hadn't even been invited. "Oh, but Katherine's here," Abby added. "She drove over from Jonesboro, you know."

This announcement was met with an approving nod from Henrietta. "Isn't that sweet. Poor Katherine had a hard time, alone the way she was after Edward died. Isn't it lucky, Abigail, that *you* have Mr. Mackintosh to help you in this time of need?"

So word was out he'd been hanging around. Reed hadn't meant for that to happen, not yet anyway.

"Yes, he's been wonderful," Abby agreed. "The children and I are very grateful."

"Why, we hear you've been going over practically every day to help Abigail with one thing or another," Henrietta said to Reed. "I'm sure Jason would be awfully pleased by the kindness you've shown."

Jason, Reed thought. Always Jason. And then he felt guilty for thinking it.

"I declare," Henrietta continued, "people are startin' to think of you as a one-man welcoming committee. I think that's sweet, don't you, Theodora?"

From the corner of his eye, Reed could see Abby's face slowly turning in his direction. "It's the least I can do...for my best friend's widow," he said, and then wished he hadn't said it in just that way.

Miss Walsh met his gaze, and Reed thought he saw a barely discernible shake of her head as though she was feeling a bit disgusted. That was all right. He was feeling plenty disgusted. And protective of Abby. He didn't want anyone—especially not these two—getting the wrong idea, that Abby was in any way being disloyal to Jason or betraying his memory or any other such nonsense. His own reputation meant nothing. But Abby's was a different story altogether.

"After all, we were...close, he and I," Reed said. "You may not remember how it was with us."

Theodora Walsh begged to differ. "On the contrary, my memory is excellent, Mr. Mackintosh. I daresay you might be surprised by all I remember."

The two women said their good evenings and walked on, leaving Reed to stand and wonder how he could possibly restore the previous mood.

"Now what do you suppose she meant by that?" Abby asked.

"Who the hell knows. Abby, I'm sorry."

"For what?"

"For referring to you as...Jason's widow."

She looked away. "It's all right, Reed. That's what I am."

"Yes, but is that all you *want* to be, damn it?"

"Of course I want to be more than that," she said evenly.

He was being defensive. A move that would hardly help matters, he knew. And she was getting angry. Reed forced himself to think clearly, to quell the emotions churning in his stomach.

"Abby, you *are* more than that," he said quietly. "A lot more. And to be honest, tonight I didn't want you reminded of that part of...things." Especially not by me, he added silently. "And if you're worried about what our two 'friends' might have seen, well...it was only a kiss, for God's sa—"

"Look, I said it's all right," she told him. But he could feel the distance between them as surely as night follows day. "Maybe it's too soon," she murmured. "Maybe people around here aren't ready to accept me as a person apart from Jason. I'm not even sure *you* are."

Reed looked up to the stars and wondered how she could possibly not know how he felt. "Oh, yes," he whispered.

"I'm ready." He faced Abby and reached for her shoulders to pull her closer. With a gentle lift of her chin, Reed looked in her eyes and went searching deep in a sea of blue. "The question is . . . are *you?*"

## *Chapter Five*

She shouldn't have done it.

Three days passed, and Abby woke up every morning to the same conclusion. She simply shouldn't have kissed Reed Mackintosh. Or let him hold her the way he had held her.

It had been a nice fit, of course. Her back against his chest. A pair of masculine arms, strong and warm around her. He had held her to him as if she was perfectly welcome to stay there. She could have. Very easily.

And therein lay the danger.

At this time, she was vulnerable, Becky had reminded her. She was a widow, her mother had reminded her. She should think hard about every decision, her father had reminded her.

She hadn't been with a man in such a long time. Of that, she needed no reminder.

On the fourth day, Abby arose from her new bed and came to the same conclusion. She shouldn't have done it.

She slipped on her robe and began pulling the sheet and spread into place. After all, the man hadn't set foot in her house since that night. Abby wondered just what she should make of that. Not that she wanted to make anything of it. Reed was obviously treating the entire incident as a casual, friendly experience.

Which was exactly what *she* was doing. More or less. The fact that he had stayed away for four days...well, friends could do that. It didn't necessarily mean anything. She hadn't seen Becky and Tom, either, and she wasn't upset about that. She wasn't upset. Just wondering. That's all. Wondering where Reed was.

Abby dressed carefully in a flowing skirt and matching rayon blouse and then hustled her daughter downstairs for breakfast. Matthew was already there pouring his second bowl of cereal.

There was a time when she would have tousled his thick, curly hair and kissed him good-morning. Since he didn't allow that anymore, Abby settled for a mild show of interest. "Sleep well, Matthew?"

He gave his usual shrug.

"What's on your agenda today?"

"Might swim at the park this afternoon."

"Sounds like fun. I hope you'll get to the lawn this morning."

"Can't. Said I'd meet some of the guys."

"Oh? What guys?"

"Frankie and..."

He seemed to be having a time coming up with additional names. She avoided mentioning the boy he had argued with the day before. Matthew had passed it off as nothing. Abby was less dismissive and would've demanded more in the way of an immediate explanation had Frankie not arrived to "hang out" with Matthew.

"Isn't Frankie working at the drugstore today?" she asked.

"Gets off at noon."

"Ah. Which should give you plenty of time to mow the lawn."

"But, Mom—"

"Save it, Matthew." She ignored his heavy sigh and set about getting toast and cereal for Molly, who chattered quietly to baby Jemima.

Matthew made ponderous work of clearing his part of the table. Bowl and spoon in turn slowly followed his glass into the dishwasher. By the time he closed the door and turned around to face her, Abby had already buttered the toast and poured a small glass of milk.

"Well?" he asked.

"Well, what, Matthew?"

"What are *you* gonna do?" he demanded to know. "I mean, you're all dressed up and everything. . . ."

"Thank you for noticing. I'm going over to Mackintosh to—"

"Can I go?" Molly asked hopefully.

Abby smiled. "Not this time. Granny Lindstrom was hoping to go on reading that bear story the two of you started last week. Finish your breakfast and I'll take you over."

Matthew leaned against the countertop and stared down at the floor. "Why are you going *there?*"

"I have a sneaking suspicion it's a job interview with Reed's father. He asked me to come in this morning to talk."

"Didn't know you wanted a job."

Abby took another sip of coffee and wished her son would speak in complete sentences. "I'm not sure I do. But maybe something on a free-lance basis. Small projects like the ones I did in Little Rock wouldn't be a bad idea."

"But you don't *have* to, do you?" he asked. "I mean, we're okay, aren't we?"

"Financially, you mean? Matthew, we're fine. Your father left us very comfortable."

"Oh, Jemima, I miss Daddy so much, don't you?" Molly hugged Jemima with five-year-old drama and rocked. "Mama, could Reed be our new daddy?"

"Are you crazy?" Matthew responded hotly. "Jeez, Molly, that's the dumbest—"

"Matthew—"

"We don't need a dad. And why does she talk to that stupid doll?"

"Hush, Matthew." Abby gave him her firmest leave-her-alone-she's-only-a-baby expression before she sat beside Molly and began adding jelly to the slice of toast. "I know you miss your father, sweetie. We all do. That's why it's very important that the three of us take extra good care of each other now. And try to understand each other," she said, looking pointedly at her son. "Understand?"

"Okay, but why don't you make her face reality? Why don't you just tell her we don't *need* another—"

"Matthew—"

"We *don't*, Mom. We don't need *anybody*," he insisted. "You oughtta tell her that once and for all. We're just fine by ourselves—just fine—and you shouldn't let her think somebody's gonna come along and take his place. Because nobody is gonna do that—you hear me? Nobody!"

Matthew wasn't fine, she knew. He had lifted his chin in contempt, but she hadn't missed the minute quiver in his lip before he regained control and gave his mouth the slightest curl.

Abby put down the bread and knife and went to him. She laid a hand on his shoulder and ignored the stiffening of his muscles. "Matthew," she said quietly, "why are you worried about someone taking your father's place? As far as I can tell, no one is even *trying* to do that. What people *are* trying to do is be your friend. Please let them, son. Please let me . . . someone."

His thick lashes lowered, and Matthew let out a ragged breath. But at least he didn't move away from her. Abby gave her son a hug, but he didn't return it. Neither did he relax. "I'll go start on the lawn," he muttered. He went out the back way and let the screen door slam before she could get to it.

Abby looked back at Molly, who had already begun explaining her brother's behavior to the ever-mindful Jemima. "He didn't mean it," she crooned. "He's just sad, that's all."

Pouring herself another cup of coffee, Abby stood at the window and looked out. *"Don't push,"* the counselor in Little Rock had said. *"Don't invade. Just listen—really listen—to his pain, his fears, and try to soothe them. But don't let him bully you. Don't let him take advantage or use his pain to get at you."*

It wasn't easy. But she was trying. And who could tell? Abby reasoned. If she got really good at this one-woman balancing act, she could take her show on the road and make millions.

Before the tears had a chance to form, Abby went upstairs to put on her jacket. She didn't want millions. She wanted happy, confident children who were at peace with themselves. Some days that goal seemed so out of reach, at least for one of her children. It would be a year come Thanksgiving that Jason had died. Here it was mid-August, and Matthew seemed no closer to accepting things, or adjusting. Likewise, Abby was no closer to figuring out a way to help him. She would be thirty-six years old next month. It seemed to Abby that at this point in her life, she ought to have figured out more than she had. At the very least, she ought to be having a better time.

As soon as Molly was safely ensconced with her grandmother, Abby drove to Mackintosh and parked the car in one of the spaces marked Visitor. The morning sun was already hot on her face as she made her way toward the entrance. Inside, the lobby was cool and softly lit. The wall behind the receptionist's U-shaped desk displayed the company logo written in bold black script on a royal blue background.

Before she could say much of anything, the young woman seated at the desk looked up and smiled. "Good morning, Mrs. Malone. Mr. Mackintosh is expecting you. Would you like coffee or a soft drink before you go in?"

When Abby declined politely, the woman pushed a few buttons on the telephone and stood. "I'll take you back then."

Even though she knew the way, Abby followed obediently. The administrative end of the business was still carried out in a huge open-plan area, which over the years had been remodeled simply by moving partitions to expand or limit space whenever the need arose.

Well aware that the noise level softened appreciably as people noticed her arrival, Abby smiled hellos to the few people she knew. Rolling up his shirtsleeves, Reed was standing a good ten feet away with his back to her. The elegant-looking blonde he was speaking to glanced up at Abby and smiled, but Reed himself didn't turn around as Abby passed. She wondered why.

She wondered all the way to Ben Mackintosh's glass-enclosed office, the first of several situated along a narrow hallway jutting off the administration area. Miniblinds, open for the moment, afforded him optional privacy, but still allowed observation of the work area.

Ben stepped to the doorway, pulled her inside and immediately closed the door after quickly thanking the receptionist. "Do you want coffee? Here, have some coffee." Since he was already pouring a cup, Abby sat down and reached for a packet of nondairy creamer.

Ben wasted no time in getting to the point. He wanted her input on their next big advertising campaign and he had already arranged everything. He ended by telling her where he had decided to put her desk.

Hardly able to take it all in, Abby was overwhelmed. "But... I can't possibly work full-time right now. I don't even want to."

"Doesn't matter to me how much you work. Don't even care if you come into the office. Do it at home or any way you want to. Just get it done." Ben leaned back in his chair and clasped his hands behind his head. "I want that department whipped into shape. With a little work, we can have a first-class—"

"But... don't you already have someone?"

He pushed out of his chair and went to the window. "Come over here." Parting two slats of the miniblinds, he pulled Abby to his side. "Over there with Reed. That Cravens woman. She's a widow, too," he added. "For a couple of years now."

"Oh," Abby said with a nod. "Does she have a first name? I mean, assuming she doesn't go by That Cravens Woman or The Widow Cravens."

"Cinda. *That's* her first name," Ben muttered edgily.

"Oh."

"Yeah, she's our 'creative director.' At least that's the title Reed gave her when he sweet-talked her away from one of those hoity-toity outfits back east. Got her master's from Boston U."

"Oh. In that case, I don't see how I could possibly be of help."

"Well, I can. So far I haven't liked a damn thing she's come up with. I want you to set her straight about what we're after. The image we want."

"Oh, dear... Look, Mr. Mackintosh—"

"Ben."

"Ben. I'm afraid I don't *know* what you're after, and even if I did, I certainly don't think I'm the one to waltz in—"

"Yes, you are. You're the perfect one. And you'll have the final say over the whole project."

Which made the matter even more alarming. This Cinda person was the one with the marketing degree...and the job title. Abby couldn't imagine being a *welcome* addition to the staff.

"Does Reed know about this plan?" she asked.

"Course he does." Ben Mackintosh shrugged. "Most of it anyway."

Abby felt a strong need to hear just exactly what part Ben's son didn't know about. Reed turned a little, enabling Ms. Cravens to see whatever was on the piece of paper he was holding. He obviously liked the woman, Abby thought, noting the way his hand went so easily to Ms. Cravens's shoulder every few moments during the conversation. But then, he wouldn't have hired her—stolen her away from another company it seemed—if he hadn't liked her.

It was even more obvious that Cinda Cravens liked Reed, judging by the way she fussed with a pearl necklace and smiled up at him as he spoke. There was a certain wistfulness in the look she gave him....

Abby broke free of the speculation. Cinda was attractive—*very* attractive—with her wispy blond hair neatly coiled into a French roll. Abby couldn't help wondering just how *much* the two of them liked each other.

"So, what do you say? Are you game?"

"I might be," Abby said, "on one condition."

"Name it."

"I don't want final say about anything at Mackintosh. But having a hand in things, a little creative input—that appeals to me very much. Maybe we could work something—"

"Come on." Ben let go of the blind and stepped to the door. "Might as well get this over with."

"Get what over with?"

"The first meeting, of course. The one where we show 'em."

"Show who what?"

"Why, we're gonna show 'em who's boss, that's what."

"Mr. Mackintosh—Ben, I think everyone around here is fairly certain who's boss," Abby said, trying hard not to smile. Was that it? Did all of this boil down to a simple father-son power struggle? If that's what it was, Abby wasn't about to get in the middle of it. She followed him reluctantly to the work area, where Ben promptly marched over and somehow situated his imposing frame between Reed and Ms. Cravens.

"Abby's here," he announced.

This time, Reed, whose frame was suddenly equally imposing, did turn around. He was surprised. Very clearly surprised, Abby noted, as if he hadn't even known she was coming.

"Hello," Abby said tentatively.

"Hello to you, too," he said with just enough calm to put Abby on guard. "Nice to see you. Have you met Cinda? She's—"

"'Course she hasn't," Ben said. "That's why I asked her here."

The smile on Reed's face tightened a bit and then disappeared altogether. "Then let me do the honors. Cinda Cravens, Abby Malone."

Abby stretched out a hand. "How do you do, Ms. Cravens."

"Hello." The handshake was friendly enough. "And please, call me Cinda."

Very gracious, Abby thought. And now that she was closer, the few tiny lines in otherwise flawless skin revealed that Cinda was probably a few years older than Abby had at first suspected.

"I asked Abby to come and talk about our advertising predicament," Ben said.

Reed snapped an impatient glance at his father. "It's hardly a predicament, Dad. And I thought we agreed that I would handle it."

"We did. But so far I haven't seen any action, so..." Ben shrugged. "I thought somebody better get on the stick. Winter'll be here before we know it. And just between you, me and the fence post, we're not ready. We've got markets to plan for, you know."

"Yes," Reed said, "I know. Cinda and I were just discussing that."

"Right," Ben said. "But from now on, I want Abby in on all discussions."

Abby felt like such an intruder. But Reed's father seemed oblivious to her discomfort or to Cinda Cravens's intense interest in the forest green carpet. When Reed's arm rose protectively to Cinda's shoulder, Abby considered backing out of the entire affair.

"Dad, I haven't had a chance to go over this with Cinda," Reed said.

"So what's to go over?" Ben insisted. "We've got Abby coming in to help out. That's all. You understand, don't you, Mrs. Cravens?"

"Yes, of course," Cinda said quietly.

The woman didn't understand at all, Abby decided. It was an exceedingly awkward foursome they made. She and Cinda with their tight little smiles. Reed and his father with barely concealed scowls. She could have pinched Ben Mackintosh. But she didn't. After all, one didn't usually assault one's prospective employer.

"You know," she remarked pleasantly, "this is all rather sudden. Maybe Cinda and I need a chance to get to know each other before—"

"Yes," Cinda said. "Why, we could go right now and have a cup of coffee somewhere. I was going to take a break anyway."

"Let's walk over to Charlie's Drugstore." Abby kept her eyes on Cinda, deliberately excluding the men from the discussion. "After all, you haven't even interviewed me for this job. We need to go over my qualifications—I might not even be right for this. And then perhaps you could show me what you have so far—I mean the direction you've taken with the campaign."

Ben nodded. "Direction is the very thing you two need to talk about." He looked at his son. "There. See? I knew it would work out."

Right, Abby thought. If one saw no need for tact, diplomacy or good employee relations, everything had worked out swimmingly.

"Son, if you want to run this company, you've gotta learn to take charge," Ben said. "Get some gumption about you."

"I can see that," Reed said dryly.

Abby felt a light clap of Ben's hand on her shoulder. "We know one guy who never had a problem with gumption, don't we?"

There it was again, Abby thought. Another ill-disguised comparison between Reed and Jason.

"Mrs. Cravens," Ben explained, "this was before your time, of course, but I know you've heard me talk about Jason Malone. Abby here was married to him and—"

"Yes, I have heard a lot about him," Cinda said politely. "It's clear he was a fine man. Abby, I don't want to rush you, but I do have another appointment in half an hour, so..."

"Ready when you are," Abby said. "Reed, I—"

"You two go ahead," he cut in, but he didn't take his eyes off Ben. "I'd like a few minutes with Dad, and then one of us will be along shortly to firm up the details."

There didn't seem to be much more to say. Abby nodded agreement and then followed Cinda to the lobby.

On the way to the drugstore, the two of them engaged in a minimal amount of small talk, but neither referred to the goings-on at Mackintosh. Abby took the opportunity to gather her thoughts and formulate questions to which she would be very interested in hearing the answers. Such as

Cinda's reasons for turning her back on a high-profile career to come to a place like Winston. Abby also wondered about her own potential contribution to the advertising campaign. Then, too, there was the possibility of a relationship between Cinda and Reed. Abby wasn't sure just why she needed to know about that. She only knew that her curiosity had definitely been aroused.

As they entered the drugstore, the bell above the door announced their arrival. After a quick greeting to Charlie and then Frankie, who appeared to be on the receiving end of a lecture about taking better care of the card rack, Abby followed Cinda to one of the red vinyl booths that had been a part of the drugstore as long as she could remember.

"Mornin', Abby. Miz Cravens. Be right with you." Mavis finished wiping down the lunch counter and then came to stand beside Abby. "Your mama and pop doin' okay these days? They haven't been in for a while."

"They're fine," Abby said. "Finishing up the last of the canning. Thanks for asking."

"Now, ya'll *do* know we don't start servin' lunch until straight up noon," Mavis said with a dip of her chin.

"Yes, we know," Abby said. "We're just here for coffee. Oh, and someone will probably join us in a few minutes."

"Uh-huh. And who might that be? If you don't mind my askin'."

"We're not sure. Either Reed or his father."

"Oh." Mavis gave her platinum blond hair a delicate pat. "In that case, y'all order anything you want. I don't mind. My gosh, I could spend all day lookin' at the Mackintosh men—either one of 'em. Besides," she added with a few lifts of heavily penciled eyebrows, "those boys really do know how to tip."

"Right," Abby said. "Now, we'll just have—"

"Don't get me wrong," Mavis rattled on. "Even though they're rich as all get-out, it makes no difference to me.

Why, if they didn't have one dollar to rub against another, they'd still get my attention."

"I'm sure they'd be flattered to hear that," Abby said. "And we'll want cream with—"

"Who in her right mind *wouldn't* be crazy about 'em?" Mavis kept right on talking. "I mean, you've got your big green eyes, a chin to die for...and that cute little lopsided grin. Oh, and just all sorts of things to make a girl go limp."

With great effort, Abby confined her response to an agreeable smile. "Just coffee, Mavis."

"Oh, all right," the waitress said with a sigh. "How about you, Miz Cravens?"

"The same for me," Cinda said.

Mavis clucked and shook her head. "And they don't even ask about the gooseberry pie." She walked away muttering something about widows "we won't mention" needing more meat on their bones.

There was a hint of disappointment in the smile Cinda aimed at the table.

"Anything wrong?" Abby asked.

"Not really. I was wondering what it's going to take for me to fit in here in Winston."

"What do you mean?"

"I mean I've been here more than a year, and so far, you and Reed are the only ones to call me by my first name. People are cordial enough," Cinda said, "but it's definitely an arm's-length friendliness."

Ben could have helped with that, Abby thought. On his recommendation alone, Cinda Cravens would've been accepted in no time at all. She wondered why he hadn't seen fit to get Cinda off to a good start.

"Can you tell me, Abby?" Cinda asked lightly. "How long does it usually take around here? To be totally accepted, that is."

"Oh, gee, knowing the Winston crowd...twenty or thirty years should do it."

Cinda took it well with a smile. "I was afraid of that."

"Here you go." Mavis set two cups of coffee and a small metal creamer on the table. "Now I'm gonna be in the back for a few minutes. If y'all need more coffee, just help yourself. And Abby, give me a holler if somebody else comes in."

"Right," Abby said. "Thanks, Mavis."

"I see *you* don't have a problem fitting in," Cinda said as soon as Mavis was out of earshot. "No wonder Ben wants you at Mackintosh. Reed tells me you're an old friend...an old family friend," Cinda clarified.

Abby nodded. "He and my husband and I grew up together. But that doesn't mean I want to take over your job."

"Frankly, I'd be glad for any help I can get. Especially since my ideas don't seem to be up to snuff, as Ben would say—as he *has* said, actually."

That was Ben, Abby thought. Always holding back. "That happens, I suppose. Artistic differences, and all that."

Cinda stopped stirring her coffee and put down her spoon. "It's more than artistic differences. Before I came to Mackintosh, I spent fifteen years running the advertising department for a major manufacturer in the east. It seems I've been trying to live it down ever since."

"Oh, I can't believe Ben would really hold that against you," Abby said. "Maybe it's a simple matter of his background being different from yours. He's an up-by-the-bootstraps kind of man who started from scratch with only a little education. He considers himself a simple man with simple needs—"

"Which he isn't at all, of course."

"But just try convincing him of that," Abby said. "But you, you're well educated and so...together. I mean, you obviously know where you're headed. You're very attractive and you have this air of confidence, of...efficiency and, oh, I don't know...elegance." Beauty, brains, competence *and* assertiveness. The more Abby talked, the more she realized just what the problem might be. Cinda Cravens scared the hell out of Ben Mackintosh. And maybe a lot of other people in Winston.

"Thanks for the compliments," Cinda said.

"You're welcome. For all the good it does."

"Right." Cinda took a deep breath and let it out again. "Even though Ben has gone along with most of the projects I've done, it's clear they're not his favorites. Not like the campaign you once came up with obviously."

"He told you about that, did he?"

"Ad nauseam." Cinda instantly put her hand on Abby's arm. "Sorry about that. It was a very clever campaign—Reed said so, too. It's just been a long week, that's all."

Considering that it was only Tuesday, Abby readily accepted the apology. Still, she wasn't at all certain what she could offer this woman, who obviously had more training, more experience and more overall knowledge of advertising than Abby did.

"Maybe what you need is a heart-to-heart with Ben," she suggested. "A friendly exchange of ideas and—"

"Believe me, I've tried to get on his wavelength," Cinda said. "I've tried to attune myself to his . . . peculiarities, so to speak."

"Oh. Well, that's good. Then if he could try to see your particular vision for Mackintosh—"

"I know," Cinda said. "But Ben Mackintosh can't seem to look past Winston, Arkansas. Honestly, sometimes I'd dearly enjoy kicking that man in the pants—that's just between you, me and the fence post, mind you."

Abby smiled. Obviously Cinda had attuned herself to one or two of Ben's favorite expressions. "You could be right. Maybe he does have trouble looking at Mackintosh in a worldwide context. But I think he would welcome a more polished image for the company if it could be done simply, without too much cockiness or conceit."

"I'm not sure I know what you're getting at."

"You have to understand that from the very beginning he's worked hard to earn and keep the goodwill of Winston. He'd rather choke than have people at home think he might be getting too big for his britches."

"Hmm. I agree that a certain amount of humility is useful from a public-image standpoint. But Abby, a successful company just has to put itself forward. Get its name out there. In marketing, self-effacement and modesty don't go very far for a growing business. And believe me, this company is bursting at the seams with new growth."

"Then the two of them must be doing something right," Abby suggested.

"Of course they are. Over half the designs we currently produce are Reed's own creations. As for Ben, I can't tell you how innovative he is when it comes to finding the best way to get things done. Line production is obviously his area of expertise." Cinda shrugged her disappointment. "I just wish he understood that marketing is mine."

It was clear that Cinda cared about the company. If Ben would only cooperate, Abby had a feeling the three of them—Cinda, Ben, and Reed—had the makings of an excellent team. The very thing Reed must have had in mind when he hired the new creative director. Cinda could definitely bring a certain amount of sophistication to the company's image. That, along with Reed's creativity and Ben's know-how, well, it all added up to great things for Mackintosh. And for Winston. Trouble was, Abby had no idea where—or even *if*—she fit into the scheme of things.

"So what do you think?" Cinda asked. "Would you like to see what the two of us can do with this project?"

"Are you sure you want me? You don't really know much about my—"

"After talking to you, I don't think it's any great risk. Anyway, Ben respects your opinion. I respect him. It's that simple."

Although she appreciated Ben's support, Abby couldn't help wondering if Reed had had anything at all to say on her behalf. Still, she wasn't about to ask.

"You know," Cinda said, "I have a feeling we're going to be friends. Good friends."

"Well, hey, we've been *great* friends for the past twenty minutes."

"And they said it wouldn't last," Cinda joked. "By the way, I met your son on Saturday."

"Oh, really?"

"And then again yesterday."

"Oh?"

"Yes. He stopped by Reed's place while I was there. Both times."

"Oh." So she saw Reed socially. That should come as no surprise, Abby supposed. So that's what he'd been up to the past few days. Hanging out with Cinda Cravens. And Matthew hadn't even mentioned being at Reed's house.

"He was there with the Benteen boy," Cinda said. "Reed's teaching Frankie some of the basics of furniture making."

"Oh."

"He hopes to get Matt interested in a project, too. Reed says he's had one or two interesting discussions with Matt. But I'm sure you know all this."

Abby answered with a noncommittal smile.

"Matt seems very bright, very perceptive. Even so, it must be difficult raising your children alone," Cinda said. "Thank God my David was already in college when my husband died."

"Oh, you have a son." A *grown* son. Abby never would have guessed. "Does he live here, too?"

"Goodness, no. Even though I was tired of crowds and high-rise apartments and back-to-back presentations, he was just getting started in a busy career. I don't think he's quite ready for the slower pace I've come to love."

"I understand Reed is the one who persuaded you to come to Mackintosh."

Cinda nodded. "He's been wonderful. Showed me around. Helped me get settled. I don't know what I would have done without him."

Reed and Cinda. Once again, Abby wondered just how close the two of them were. Once again, she didn't want to think about the possibilities.

"Actually, the move has probably helped me a lot more than I've helped the company," Cinda said. "And of course, Reed's done everything he could to launch me into polite society," she teased. "Alas..."

"Alas what?" Reed asked. Abby hadn't even heard the bell.

"Reed, you made it." Stating the obvious, Cinda moved over to make room for him in the booth. "I was just telling Abby how I haven't quite 'taken' yet in Winston."

"Of course you have." He sat down beside Cinda and gave Abby a wink. "When Cinda first came to town, the farmers would circle her a couple of times before they said hello, but I don't think they do that anymore. I call that progress."

Cinda laughed and shook her head. "He's exaggerating, but only a little."

"And you have to admit," Reed observed, "that at the last town picnic, they did let you bring the potato salad."

"Now, I do call *that* progress," Abby said. "People around here are fussy about their picnics."

"Then I suppose I should be flattered," Cinda said. "What did you usually bring to these events, Abby?"

"I can't even recall the last time I attended a town picnic," she said, "much less what I brought in the way of food."

"Raisin crisscross pie," Reed said, "the summer I joined the air force." He leaned back against the seat and let out a reminiscent sigh. "That pie was heaven."

"That's right. It was pie," Abby said, thinking back. "But how do you remember? Especially when the whole thing—pie plate and all—was stolen before anyone had a chance to slice— Reed Mackintosh, were you the one?"

Reed leaned forward and rested his arms on the table. "Like I said, it was heaven."

"But . . . why?"

There was a look of unabashed guilt on his face. Still, he offered no explanation.

"Maybe he just loves raisin pie?" Cinda suggested, and then she looked at her watch. "I'm going to be late if I don't leave this instant."

Reed got up and let her out of the booth. "Did you two come to some sort of understanding?"

Cinda nodded. "I'd like the chance to work with Abby. If she's agreeable to it, the two of you can work out the details. Her ideas make a lot of sense."

"Good," Reed said. "I'll be interested to hear them."

Abby fought hard not to make something of the affectionate sidelong hug he gave his creative director. When Cinda set a dollar bill on the table, he returned it to her hand and wrapped her fingers around the money. "This one's on me."

"Thanks. See you back at the office later?" Cinda asked him.

He nodded. As soon as Cinda was on her way, Reed went behind the counter and helped himself to a cup of coffee. "A refill, Abby?"

"No, thanks." She made a concentrated effort not to follow the movement of his shoulders or his hips or his hands or any other memorable parts of his body as he returned to sit across from her again.

"So, Abby, tell me about your ideas."

"So, Reed, tell me about my pie."

"Hell, who remembers? It was all such a long time ago. . . ."

"I think you remember well enough," she said. "And someday I'm going to demand a full accounting, Reed Mackintosh."

"And someday you'll probably get it. Now, about those ideas?"

He was obviously in a hurry to change the subject, and Abby decided to let him. "I'd rather not get into specifics without seeing what's been done so far, but in a nutshell, it looks as if we'll be going for something akin to chic without arrogance—the last thing we want to do is appear uppity, you know."

"That approach is sure to make Dad happy."

"I thought so. What about you, Reed? Tell me what approach will make you happy?"

Reed gave her a searching stare. Then his gaze dropped to the tabletop. For a long moment, he studied a spoon, tracing the shape with a fingertip before he finally looked at her again and spoke softly. "Somehow, I don't think my happiness lies in an advertising campaign, Abby."

"I was thinking of all your designs."

"There aren't that many. What about them?"

"Cinda says more than half are yours. You deserve some individual recognition for—"

"Don't need it," he said. "My mark on my custom pieces is all the recognition I want. By the way, thanks for being so cooperative with Cinda. Lately, Dad hasn't made things easy for her."

"So I hear. How about you, Reed?"

"What do you mean?"

"It doesn't look as if he's making things easy for you, either."

Reed waved away the notion. "Dad is Dad. He never changes."

"But the subtle comparisons to Jason...that must bother you."

"No," he said. "Not really. Look, Abby—"

"And I don't remember his being so critical, even when he had something to be critical about."

Reed almost laughed. "Then you weren't paying attention. But I have a lot to make up to him, Abby."

"Haven't you done that? The constant reminders... Reed, that was then. This is now," she said. "You're not the same person who—"

"I do like to think I've grown up some," he said dryly.

"Well, then, shouldn't you say something to him?"

He shook his head.

"Why not?"

"I don't see any need to—"

"Don't see any need? I don't get it, Reed."

"Abby, I really don't want to talk about—"

"Don't you want to do something to—"

"Yes," he said, "I do. And what I'd like to do is drop it."

"But—"

"I mean it, Abby. Damn it, just stay out of it."

Well. She felt as if she had been very firmly put in her place. She didn't much like the feeling, either. Reed sat back and played with the spoon again.

"How's Matt?" he asked finally.

"You tell me," she said tartly. "You seem to spend more time with him than I do. I hear he was at your house twice last week. Something he didn't bother to share with me." Her tone was cutting enough to bring the slightest curve to his mouth.

"You wouldn't be jealous, would you?"

"No," she said evenly, "I'm not jealous."

"Are you sure?"

"Yes."

"I think you are."

"I am not."

"Are, too."

"Am not."

"Are, too."

"Am—" Abby stopped herself, her throat bubbling with laughter at her own peevishness. How did he do it? she wondered. Make her angry one minute and have her laughing at herself the next. But when she felt Reed's hand cover hers on the tabletop, her throat constricted a bit, stilling any other questions she might have had.

"Abby, I'm sorry."

"For what?"

"For being so abrupt. I didn't mean to hurt your feelings."

"You didn't hurt my feelings."

"Did, too."

"Did n—" She gave him a patient sigh. "Okay, you hurt my feelings. A little. But it's all right. I'm a big girl, and I can take it."

This time she got the full effect of "that cute little lop-sided grin" Mavis had mentioned. "That's my Abby," he said.

Before she could assure him that she was hardly *his* Abby, his green eyes fixed intently on her face, stealing her breath as well as her resolve. And then there was his chin—what had Mavis said? To die for? Mavis was absolutely right, Abby decided. It was almost too much to bear, all that and the easy glide of his finger along her thumb.

She let out a slow breath and realized she should think seriously about moving her hand. Curiously, Abby found herself reluctant to break the contact. She gave his fingers a gentle squeeze, friendly at first and then...less casual, more affectionate. Good grief, what was she doing holding his hand?

"Why, Abby Malone," Mavis said, letting go of the swinging door, "what do you think you're doing?" Abby had already pulled free of Reed's grasp by the time the waitress got around the counter and moved toward the booth. "You were supposed to tell me if anyone else came

82

82 HUSBAND IN WAITING

Reed's direction.

"Well, he got his own coffee and . . . it simply slipped my
mind," Abby said, feeling the brush of Reed's leg under the
table as both his feet captured one of her ankles.

"Oh, well, no harm done," Mavis said. "What can I get
you, Reed honey?"

"Another cup of your great coffee would be nice," he
suggested.

A wide grin spread across Mavis's face and she looked at
Abby. "Isn't he just the sweetest thing?"

"Adorable," Abby said dryly. She sipped her coffee and
tried to free her foot without alerting the entire Western
Hemisphere. His stare was unswerving and shameless. Abby
could see that any attempt at escape was useless at this
point.

"A pretty good dancer, too," Mavis added. "You
shoulda seen him and Miz Cravens at the Red Rooster last
month. Y'all still goin' over there, Reed?"

"Now and then."

"Hmm-hmm," the waitress said. "This wouldn't be get-
tin' serious, would it?"

"Mavis, you know I take my dancing very seriously."

"Now *that* wasn't what I—humph," Mavis said with a
good-natured slap of his shoulder. "You've never been one
to kiss and tell anyway."

Maybe not, Abby thought, looking away. But all in all it
was one more reminder that Reed Mackintosh had always
liked women. Lots of women. And oh, how they liked him
back. But these days, for some reason, it was beginning to
annoy Abby as it never had before. She was too old to be
taken as one among many. She had a feeling she had always been too old—or too something—for that kind of
game.

"On second thought, I think we'll forget the coffee,"
Reed said to Mavis. And then he looked at Abby. "I've got

to be someplace in the next half hour. Would you mind coming with me? We could finish our business on the way."

"What business?" Mavis asked the question at the same time Abby did.

"Haven't you heard?" Reed said to the waitress. "Abby's going to work at Mackintosh."

"Really," Mavis said. "Well, isn't that nice."

"We think so," Reed replied. "She'll be working at home most of the time. But we haven't settled the details yet. Maybe you could make us some sandwiches and we could work through lunch."

"Well, of course I can," Mavis said. "Let's see, we've got tuna on rye, roast beef, naturally, and hot ham and cheese. . . ."

"One of each," Reed decided. "Abby, is that all right with you?"

Was what all right? she wondered. Business? The drive? Hot ham and cheese?

"Sure," she agreed, not feeling sure at all.

"We'll stop for wine," he whispered. "Something that goes with business."

Mavis had already turned away. "Uh-huh. Sounds more like monkey business to me, folks."

Abby heard the bell over the drugstore door and looked up in time to see her son holding the door for a young girl, who preceded him into the store. After several moments of looking around—for Frankie, no doubt—Matthew finally caught sight of Abby.

"Mom," he said, obviously surprised, "what are you doing here?"

The blond-haired girl followed him over and stood a little behind him. It was then Abby noticed that Matthew had recently showered. His hair had been carefully combed, and he smelled suspiciously of after-shave.

"I've been talking with the creative director at Mackintosh," Abby said, "and Reed, of course." She gave the girl a smile and received an attractively shy one in return. "Did you find time for the lawn this morning, son?"

"Yes, Mother, I took care of that," he said so seriously that Abby was fascinated with this new and unexpected maturity, even if it didn't sound much like his real voice. "I mowed the lawn, bagged the clippings, trimmed, etcetera."

Bagged the clippings? Matthew? And what was this etcetera business? Abby wanted to look at Reed and see if he was as impressed as she was, but she didn't dare.

"Mom and...uh, Reed," Matthew said, "this is Carrie Alexander. We're just hanging out together 'til Frankie's done."

"Oh. How nice to meet a friend of Matthew's," Abby said. A nice, *gracious* friend, she thought, when Carrie very naturally shook Abby's outstretched hand and said hello to her and Reed.

"Well, she isn't really *my* friend," Matthew explained nervously. "I mean...well, she's my friend, too, but what I mean is, she's more Frankie's...friend than mine...I guess."

"I see," Abby said with a nod. He was obviously crazy about Carrie, who was so much more self-assured than he was and much more at ease.

"Carrie, it's nice to see you again," Reed said, "no matter whose friend you are. Tell your folks I said hi, would you?" he asked with such charm that the girl readily agreed.

Matthew stood awkwardly for a moment and then shrugged. "I guess we'll go find Frankie and—"

"Hey, Matt," Reed said, "I've been meaning to talk to you about something. It's about time for you to start learning how to drive. I'll have some free time in the next few weeks. I know your dad would have wanted to be the one to teach you, but—"

"Would he?" Matthew asked in a tone that Abby had so hoped would be long gone by now. But his entire manner had changed at the mention of Jason.

"Yes, I think he would have," Reed said. "Anyway, I've got a Mustang that doesn't get a lot of exercise. We could take it out sometime when you have an hour or so and—"

"Thanks, but I'm kinda busy and—"

"Why, Matthew, what a great offer," Abby said. "I'm sure you could find some time for—"

Her son was shaking his head. "Thanks, but I don't think so. I got school coming up and . . . stuff to do at home."

"Right," Reed said, but Abby could see the disappointment in his eyes. "If you change your mind, I'm here. You know, your dad and I were good friends and I'd consider it the least I can do for his son."

None of Reed's words carried any weight with Matthew, Abby noticed. He looked away and closed up tighter than ever. Fortunately, Mavis came just then with the sandwiches. Reed spent several moments praising her efforts and then hustled Abby toward the door, leaving Mavis to deal with Carrie and Matthew.

# Chapter Six

"I thought we had to be somewhere."

"We did. And this is where we had to be. I thought you might like it here."

"I do," Abby said. "I like it very much."

She held her skirt close and bent down to the edge of the river, letting the water rush a pleasant coolness through her fingers. The relatively tame stretch of rapids was like soothing distant thunder to her ears.

Abby wasn't exactly sure how she had come to be standing on the bank of the Buffalo River. Especially since she had planned to run errands and shop for a bread box after her appointment with Ben. She only knew that after the one stop for a bottle of chilled chardonnay, Reed had driven her and the sandwiches straight to this shady spot, where cottonwoods mingled amiably with the willows and river birch, all leaning out over the water to form leafy parasols for the occasional canoe bobbing idly along the Buffalo.

A little bit of heaven, she thought, looking to the opposite bank and up past the treetops to the cotton-and-blue sky.

"What do you think, Abby? Is it the way you remember it?"

"Oh, yes. Even better than I remember it."

So far, not one word about business or the terms of her employment had been mentioned. Not in the car and not in this place where she and her parents had come with the Mackintosh family so many times before the death of Reed's mother.

Abby stood and sipped from the paper cup of wine he had poured for her. What fun she'd had with him then. Hiking the trails. Scrambling up the paths to the overlook. Camping. Canoeing. Even when the river was at its lowest, as it was now, they still managed to have a good time together.

But then Mrs. Mackintosh had died. Abby couldn't remember ever coming back to this particular spot after that. Reed had more or less claimed it as his own, and he had never invited her.

Standing very close, he touched a breeze-blown strand of her hair and smoothed it away from her face. His palm lingered on her cheek, and he stared intently into her eyes for a moment before letting go and moving away a little. "Are you sure you don't want something more to eat?" he asked. "You hardly touched your sandwich."

"I'm fine. I'd forgotten how beautiful it is here."

"My favorite place in the world," he said.

She knew. As a teenager, Reed had disappeared for days at a time to camp on this very spot, sometimes with Jason or other boys, but more often alone.

"We had fun here, didn't we, Abby?"

"Yes, we did. That is, until you made it a males-only camp, off-limits to girls—to *this* girl anyway."

He nodded. "I do remember asking Jason not to bring you here."

"I know. I never understood why I wasn't welcome, though."

"Maybe I just didn't want you to come here with any other guy except me."

"Right," she said, laughing her disbelief. Abby had seen it as rejection then. And that was pretty much the way she saw it now. Funny how the knowledge could still hurt. "I figured it had to be one of those *guy* things."

"Oh, yes," he admitted with the slightest smile, "you can be sure it was one of those *guy* things." His gaze at the water was wistful, but after a moment, he seemed to shake the feeling off. "Want to get your feet wet? We could wade downstream for a way." He sat on a large flat rock and reached down to untie his shoes.

"In my stockings?"

"Take them off," he suggested.

The shallow rapids did look inviting. Abby had already removed her jacket and left it in Reed's car. While he finished rolling the cuffs of his pants up to the middle of his calves, she stepped out of her pumps and turned away, lifting her skirt to remove her panty hose.

When she returned, Reed had filled her cup again, and she took it with her to the water's edge. He came to stand behind her, slipping his arms around her waist to pull her against him. "It's just you and me today," he said. "I have to say I like that."

"Me, too," she agreed. And still she pulled away with the excuse of setting her cup beside his on the rock. After returning to the edge of the water, Abby kept some distance between them, knowing that, with no trouble at all, his arms would become too comfortable, too cozy, if she were to sweep caution aside and let them. Rounded pebbles teased her toes as cold water moved over them and covered her feet. "You haven't been around lately, Reed. Any special reason?"

"Have you missed me?"

Abby gave him the slightest shrug. "Maybe. Actually, I've been too busy to give it a lot of thought."

"That isn't very flattering."

It wasn't very truthful, either. Not if she counted the nights she'd lain awake until all hours thinking about him.

"I don't want to crowd you, Abby. Thought maybe you'd want some time to get settled, just you and your kids. But if you've had enough, I'd love to see you—all of you—more often. Although I'm not so sure your son would welcome the prospect."

"Reed, I'm sorry about Matthew and the way he behaved. I—"

"You don't need to apologize, Abby. He's simply not ready yet to—"

"Act like a human being?" she suggested.

He let out a low chuckle that Abby found thoroughly charming. "He does seem to run hot and cold where I'm concerned. But I hope he'll keep coming around to the workshop at least."

Reed was touching her again. But this time it was a casual, friendly hand that had slipped around her waist and was rocking her with gentle movements. The motion lulled her senses until a certain tenderness spread softly inside her.

As he brought a rough-soft jaw next to her face, she felt a growing contentment mingled with an edge of excitement. "If you look through those trees across the river, you'll get a glimpse of a barbed-wire fence and the field beyond," he said. "Remember the time the bull chased us out of his pasture?"

"Of course I do. I was the first one back to camp, as I recall."

"Well, yes, but only because a man has a duty to stay behind and protect his womenfolk."

Despite his teasing, Abby knew that something was going on between them. Something she wasn't at all certain about. But the years were there all around them, the memories giving her confidence one moment, taking it away the next.

"Same thing happened to me and Jason," he reminisced. "Damned if he didn't beat me back to camp, too. Guess you two were a match even then."

He was wrong. Still, Abby stood silently, sharing the past with Reed. They had gone through a happy childhood together, a sometimes difficult adolescence, and then moved right on into adulthood. Together. During the ups, the downs, the comings and goings of families and friends. And through it all, she had felt a connection to him that she had never known with anyone else, not even Jason. At times, she had certainly felt closer to Reed. Although she wasn't sure why. Maybe she *was* "his Abby," after all, she decided. Had always been, in one way or another. At least it made her feel better to think so. She savored the memories, letting them surround her with warmth and affection for him. She remembered the warmth and affection she had once felt for Jason.

The tear that dropped onto her cheek rather stunned her at first. Abby hadn't even been aware of the sadness welling deep within her. She quickly wiped the droplet away.

"What is it, Abby?"

"I don't know." And she didn't know. But when his arms went around her, she found herself wanting, needing them to stay there. "Just thinking, I guess...about things." Abby breathed carefully to still the trembling in her voice. "About the way my life—*our* lives have gone. How time keeps passing so fast, and we take wrong turns and make wrong choices...and how we go along and get along, but not without pain and so much waste in the process..." Abby turned in his arms and tried hard to swallow the tears. "I've come to realize that I was no match at all for Jason," she said. "I wasn't the right woman for him." Well aware of the doubt in his eyes, Abby sighed and shook her head. "Why should that surprise you, Reed? You've been searching for years and haven't found the right woman."

"Yes, but maybe there's a good reason for that," he said softly.

Abby smiled. "Of course there is. You always did like the hunt better than the capture." His mouth took on a grim line. She hadn't meant to annoy him. But truth was truth. They had known each other too long to have it any other way. "You've been so much a part of my life and . . . I've missed you, Reed."

"Abby," he murmured. Now he was the one who seemed stunned. She could see the wonder, the caution, in his eyes as he reached up and pressed a gentle thumb to her wet cheek. "I know you've been through hell."

She had. Even so, there was more to it than that. Much more.

"Those must have been lonely times," he added, "what with Jason's work and all. And then nursing him through the last year."

Yes. Lonely and bitter. But not because of her husband's work. Not even because of his illness. She wasn't certain she wanted Reed to know that. Not that or the crazy shame she herself had felt over Jason's affair, the humiliation of not seeing, not knowing about something that had been going on right under her nose for years.

Reed was still stroking her cheek, but Abby couldn't look at him. "Tell me something," she said. "About that night. That last night you visited us in Little Rock."

"What is it?" His question was full of caution.

Still she needed to know. "Was it because of the woman?"

"What woman?"

"The one who came with you when you brought Jason back to the house. I know he'd had too much to drink and he was being obnoxious, but—"

"Abby, please, let's not go over this a—"

"But I need to, Reed. I need to go over this. I need to know if you hit him because of her. I mean the two of you left the house as friends, but when you came back with that woman—"

"It was just a crazy, stupid argument," he insisted. "God, I don't even remember her name."

Abby did. She would never forget it. "So you didn't know her before?"

He waited, obviously weighing the question, maybe his answer, too. Finally, Reed sighed. "No, I didn't know her."

Abby nodded. For the longest time, she had wanted to blame Reed for at least part of Jason's infidelity. Somehow, believing that it wasn't *all* Jason's fault, that his best friend had introduced the two of them and even encouraged Jason to be unfaithful, had made the whole thing easier to bear. But only a little. Abby couldn't recall exactly when she had come to her senses and put the responsibility back on her husband where it belonged.

"Did you know that eventually she went to work in Jason's office?" she asked.

This time Reed looked away. "No, I didn't know that."

The two of them stood in silence. The breeze off the water cooled her face and eased her thoughts a little. She believed that Reed hadn't known the woman before that night. Still, Abby wondered how much he *did* know. Or maybe he had only suspected.

His fingers caressed and soothed. Yet she hesitated to say more to this man who had loved Jason, too.

"Abby," he coaxed, "tell me what's bothering you. Tell me. Maybe I can help."

She let out a long breath and knew no one could do that. "They had an affair, Reed. A long and apparently... loving one."

Reed's hands had stilled on her skin. Her eyes stung the way they always did when she tried to sort out the past with

Jason. Abby looked up to the disbelief she knew she would see in Reed's eyes.

"Yes, I'm sure," she offered before he could ask. "Jason confessed a month or so into his illness."

"Just had to get it off his chest, did he?"

The tightness in Reed's lips left her own mouth trembling. He had let go of her to run his fingers harshly through his hair. Abby felt a reminiscent rejection before he mercifully came close again and held her.

"I'm sorry, Abby. So sorry. I know you loved him."

She gave him a small smile full of regret. "Apparently not in the way he wanted to be—"

"Stop," he said, and lifted her chin so that she had to look at him. "Don't do that. Don't take his guilt and make it your own. Don't let him hoist his own burden onto your shoulders." He shook his head. "What the hell happened to him? What could he have been thinking to turn his back on you for another woman?"

"It...wasn't the first time," she said, hanging on to Reed for the support she dearly needed at that moment. "There were others before her."

"He told you that?"

She nodded.

"My God. What did you say? What did you do?"

Abby shrugged a resignation she didn't feel at all. "What do you—what *can* you—say to a man who's dying? A man you've loved. A man you've had children—" Abby stopped, each admission bringing more pain than the one before it. She didn't think she could say much more. Neither could she stand the disappointment, the bitterness, she saw in Reed's eyes. "I didn't tell you these things to hurt you," she said. "I know you loved him. I just needed to tell someone who knew him the way you did, someone who would understand."

He stared for some time, his gaze searching her face, before he spoke again. "I know. And I do understand."

Abby expelled a long, slow breath of relief. "Look, I didn't expect to get into this today. In fact, I never expected to get into it at all, but—"

"It's okay, Abby. You needed to talk. I'm glad to be the one you chose to talk to."

"I hope I haven't completely ruined—"

"You haven't ruined anything. Now stop apologizing. Let's move on. Deal?" he asked, and actually smiled at her.

"Deal," she answered.

Reed left a feathery kiss on her nose and motioned toward the water. "Shall we?"

Even as she nodded, Abby wondered if he could really move on so easily. She wasn't certain at all that she could. Still she owed it to Reed to give it her best shot. At least for the rest of the afternoon.

Abby bunched her skirt and held it high above her knees.

"Careful," Reed said, unable to deny himself a quick glance at the length of exposed thigh that moved beside him as he took her hand and led her deeper into the clear water.

So Abby had come home to heal, he reasoned. To take stock. To remember better times with Jason. Friendship. That was all she wanted from Reed. It made him angry that even in death Jason was there between them. Angry that Abby would allow it. And what would she do when she was done healing? Leave again? Leave him? *Again?*

Jason had cheated Abby out of a good marriage, a good life. Reed wanted to thrash him even now. He remembered the night he *had* thrashed Jason. The night that the two of them had gone into the club and found the woman waiting. When Jason had asked him to cover for him—to lie to Abby!—so that he could . . .

Reed swallowed, unable to stomach the thought of his friend's betrayal . . . and Abby's ensuing anger when Reed hit Jason. He couldn't tell her his reasons at the time, just as he couldn't find it in himself to tell her today. Now, here he was again, playing the friend. He wasn't sure how long he could do that. Or even *if* he could do it.

True to her promise to move on, Abby was teasing him with small, delicate splashes of water to his chest. When she did that, it took every ounce of his self-control not to sweep her into his arms right then and there to show her how he really felt.

But as Abby smiled expectantly up at him, sending a surge of longing through his groin, Reed found himself helpless in the glow of her lighter mood. He would find a way to be her friend. He was powerless to do anything else.

"Let's go that way," she said, motioning toward a shaded cove where water trickled down an algae-covered embankment.

Reed seemed agreeable enough to her suggestion, Abby noted, silently thanking him for listening, then so easily lifting her spirits. But then he had always been able to do that.

Maneuvering over the gravel bottom was easy enough. However, the going became more difficult among the slippery, larger rocks that lay in the faster flow. Abby picked her way carefully beside him to a knee-high depth in the rapids. There she stopped for a moment to lift her hair off her neck and let the cool breeze soothe her skin. Several deep breaths of the clean, moist air filled her lungs before she allowed him to coax her forward again.

Having her hand in his larger, sturdier one felt very right and natural to Abby as she waded cautiously downstream with Reed. Along the way, he alerted her to a couple of great blue herons keeping vigil at the top of a cypress tree. A kingfisher swooped down out of nowhere, it seemed, to pluck a fish from the water just yards in front of her.

Abby watched the bird's ascent back to its perch before she lost track of it and turned her attention to other sights and sounds in the woods beyond. The skies were clear, with brilliant rays of sunshine slanting through the trees.

While she was aware of much of the activity in and out of the river, Abby was most conscious of the man moving beside her. His green eyes, guarded by dark brows, crinkled at the corners each time he looked up to the treetops. His steps were less cautious than hers, more confident. The cuffs of his pants were already soaked, but he was doubtless oblivious of that fact.

Reed maintained a leisurely pace, stopping now and then to fasten his gaze on an interesting plant or tree on the shore. Entwining his fingers in hers, he pulled her along, tightening his hold when she faltered, relaxing his grip when she regained her footing. Now and then he bent low, his shoulder brushing hers, his face almost touching her cheek, to point out a crayfish or some other form of water life.

Her attention was drawn to a patch of shade near the shore where a female wood duck swam with five baby ducklings in tow. Ripples of water fanned out from the line as the mother led her children past driftwood and floating leaves. Standing as still as possible, Abby squeezed Reed's hand and motioned toward the quiet pool of water.

"A daily constitutional," she whispered.

"Nah, she's definitely taking the brood out to lunch," he whispered back.

Abby moved out of his grasp, inching her way in front of him for a closer look. Not wanting to scare the birds away, she stopped just to his right, reluctant to approach any nearer.

All at once, the rock she stood on shifted, throwing Abby off balance. Her feet went out from under her, and the resulting splash brought forth a breathless squeal as she sat in icy water that immediately penetrated her clothing and swirled uncharitably around her waist. A few moments of thrashing about only served to douse the front of her blouse before Reed grabbed hold and pulled her up into his arms to smooth her hair away from her face.

"Are you all right?" he asked looking down, his concern tinged with amusement.

"Great," she said with a shiver. "Just great." She looked at her hands, which were now as wet as her clothes, and wondered what she would use to dry the water clinging to her face.

Reed said nothing, but raised a dry palm to gently wipe her cheeks and eyelids.

"Thanks."

"My pleasure."

In a moment of sheer giddiness, Abby settled her arms ever so casually around his neck. "Well, I guess I took care of any snakes or other vermin that might be lurking around."

"I don't know about that," he said, "but you certainly scared the hell out of the wood ducks."

Her head dropped back in laughter as she pictured the indignant ducklings scattering in all directions. Abby stood in the water with Reed, and as the giggling faded, she let out an affectionate sigh and looked up into his eyes again.

"At least *you* didn't abandon me," she said, her voice still breathy from all the commotion.

"How could I?" he asked, tracing a finger along her lower lip. "Now it really *is* just you and me. For the very first time, I feel as if I really do have you all to myself."

Abby couldn't deny she liked the sound of that. Even though having a cast of thousands would have been safer. With an audience, he wouldn't have been touching her the way he was, fanning his fingers through her hair, or looking at her with such...intent. And she definitely wouldn't have been this feverish as he pulled her toward him.

His lips touched hers in a tender prelude, tasting first in one corner and then pressing lightly into the other. It took no time at all for her breathing to crescendo again. Abby couldn't remember feeling this way for such a long time. Yes, an audience would have been much safer.

"Abby," he groaned desperately. Then Reed hauled her up to him, and his mouth covered hers in hot temptation, coaxing, nipping, caressing, numbing her lips and her senses. He let his tongue move back and forth in a merciless taunt before slipping it inside for a sensuous duel. Then he captured her mouth completely.

There was a gentle strength in the way he held her. The faintest moan escaped her, and a fundamental weakness overcame her knees. And still his mouth moved over her face, down her neck, before scorching a slow path to her lips again.

For long, languorous moments, she reveled in all the sensations that had long been denied her. Big hands palmed her back at first, but then worked their way slowly down to her hips, coaxing her even closer with impassioned desire.

Her breasts grew warm with wanting. At the back of his neck, her fingers dipped below his collar and treated themselves to slow strokes of his nape before entwining the thick, dark strands of his hair. Moving around to the front of his shirt, she let her hands slide beneath the now-damp cotton to explore the muscled planes of his chest.

His thigh pressed into her, and she knew a primitive longing. Her heart began to beat faster, and through the wet blouse and bra, her breasts strained for the pleasure of his touch. As though sensing her need, he reached under her shirt, and pushing aside all barriers, he cupped one breast and sent a taunting thumb to tease the nipple into a tight, pulsating peak. The circular motion sent ripples of yearning through Abby. The chill in her skin was gone now, replaced by the hot tide of passion.

She had long ago abandoned attempts to hold the hem of her skirt out of the water. The material clung to her legs in wet folds, and Reed gathered a bunch of it in one hand and began a most tantalizing slide up her thigh. All the possibilities of what might be about to happen settled on Abby in one astounding reality.

"Reed, I...we...can't...do this. Not yet. I just can't."

He tore his mouth from hers and breathed onto her cheek, but he didn't let go. "I know, Abby. I know. Just let me stay here a little longer. Kissing you. Being close to you, loving you...just a little longer...just..." A ragged moan issued from him before he pressed his lips to her throat and then moved up to take her mouth again.

His hand splayed across her bare thigh and coaxed her leg around his. When he cupped her hip and pressed her to him, Abby instinctively responded with equal and glorious pressure. Each time he moved against her, the realization of what she was doing both amazed and alarmed her. The rightness. The wrongness. The danger, the rapture. She thought she'd lost her mind for all the control she displayed.

Abby could feel her resolve quickly fading, her reason hanging by a thread. She sensed his determination growing with each masculine stroke of her thigh. She summoned one last bit of emotional strength and wrenched free of his mouth and pushed away from his chest.

"Reed, please, don't," she said between heavy breaths. "This isn't right. This isn't the way I—" But it was very right, she knew. At least, the idea of it was. And if she was honest, it was a most excellent way....

"All right," he murmured. He held her close again and stroked her hair. "All right, Abby, we won't. Not this time."

His chest heaved with each breath, soothing her in the same way a gentle rocking might settle a child. She accepted his support, hanging on for several more moments of splendor in the strength and shelter he gave.

When at last her own heartbeat had calmed, he led her out of the water and onto the shore. Reed turned her to him and stared hungrily down at her, apparently reluctant to let her go just yet. Abby bit her lip and wondered crazily if it was too late to change her mind. But Reed was already straightening her clothing. He buttoned her blouse and was in the

process of smoothing the collar into place when he stopped
and raked a rough hand across his mouth and jaw.

Letting out a slow breath, he pressed a gentle kiss to her
lips and sighed. "We'd better go while I still can."

Abby nodded and reached for her shoes. "Reed, your
shirt's all wet. You should take it off and—"

"Hey, I will if you will."

She gave no sign of the temptation she felt.

"Abby, you're blushing."

Well, maybe a small sign.

"You're the one who needs to get out of your clothes,"
he said. "You can wear my jacket."

Upon consideration, Abby thought not.

"It's in the car," he said. "My jacket, I mean."

So was hers. She didn't answer.

"Abby, do you have a problem with that?"

She very definitely had a problem with that. Mainly she
feared that once she got her clothes off, she might not be
willing to put anything—his jacket or hers or anyone
else's—back on. Not for a while anyway.

"I'll just . . . keep my shirt on, thank you."

"What's the matter? Don't you trust yourself?"

This time she made certain he couldn't see her face. "Of
course I trust myself. Haven't you noticed? I'm heavy into
self-control."

"No," he said thoughtfully. "You're heavy into something, but it isn't control."

"Oh?" She walked ahead of him toward the car. "Well,
what do *you* think it is?"

"I'm not sure, but I think they call it denial."

She was *not* in denial. Abby had no idea *what* she was in.
Trouble came instantly to mind. She knew one thing. She
had no business getting involved with Reed Mackintosh, not
in the way she was considering. If Abby had learned one
thing over the years, it was that a leopard couldn't change

his spots. And neither could Reed Mackintosh. He was only trying to help her start over, help her and her family feel comfortable in Winston. It was her own fault if his help, his comfort were making her think all kinds of silly thoughts. And oh, she did feel silly. And foolish. And giddy.

And scared.

A few days passed before Abby began forcing herself to think practically. Okay, there was a definite attraction between them. Probably nothing more than lust. That was all. Lust. Not love. She liked to think she still knew the difference.

For the longest time, she hadn't even been out with a man, except for Douglas Canfield, Jason's partner, who had bought out his interest in the medical practice. But she could hardly count a few dinners and some well-meaning brotherly advice—some considerably *older* brotherly advice—as any kind of relationship. She was most likely lonely, but that was probably all it was.

And then there was Reed to think about. Commitment was hardly a word she had ever associated with him. At least not in the romance department.

All through high school his name had never been linked with any one female for more than one semester. And later, well . . . Abby couldn't count the times he had shown up on her and Jason's doorstep with a different woman. Reed Mackintosh had a reputation as a womanizer. A very handsome, lovable, but notorious womanizer.

Abby knew that. Had *always* known that. And yet she couldn't dismiss her attraction. Her desire. Feelings that took her very breath every time she thought about them. Yes, there was something special between them. She just wasn't sure what it was.

During the following week, she occupied her time with mornings at Mackintosh, afternoons of last-minute shopping for school clothing and supplies, enrolling Matthew and Molly for the fall term, and generally giving her children pointers on life in a small-town school. She was certain those helpful hints rolled off Matthew's back and splatted somewhere on the floor behind him. Molly was much more receptive and *biddable,* as Reed pointed out generously and often.

Although she invited Reed to dinner once and saw him at odd intervals here and there, Abby took care to keep their private time together brief and subject to invasion at any moment. If it bothered Reed, he gave no sign of it, but instead seemed perfectly agreeable to almost every situation, including a trip to Clarksville to attend a matinee of *Snow White* with her and Molly. He very gallantly held Abby's hand as well as her daughter's throughout the poison-apple scene and beyond.

But at night alone in her bed, Abby let down her guard and gave way to blissful attempts to define not what she *had* with Reed, but what she fancied *having* with this man. Nearly every one of her dreams of him began with more cerebral pursuit of a viable ad campaign. But sooner or later, fantasy took over and, to her utter frustration, transformed the nocturnal struggle into glorious, crowning passion between them.

All in all, she found the emotional exercise exhausting. Especially since every morning she awoke no closer to a civilized solution to loneliness, or any other questions her heart had been asking lately.

"You're looking a little peaked," Becky said one morning after Abby had deposited Molly at school and stopped by the inn for a chat. "Something keeping you awake nights?"

Abby stirred the cream in her coffee. "I'm all right. Things have been hectic lately. That's—"

"It's a man, isn't it?"

"Now why on earth would you—"

"You've got all the signs, that's why. And Abby, I think it's positively wonderful. But who? I didn't even know you'd been out with anyone except—"

"Becky, it isn't what you—"

"Oh, no. Not Reed. Tell me it isn't Reed Mackintosh."

Abby shifted uncomfortably.

"Oh, Abby, no. I'm all for your getting back in the race, but did you have to start with someone so...challenging...so...?"

"I know."

"Is it serious?"

"Of course n—"

"Oh, *Abby*. You and he haven't...you know. Have you?"

"No, we haven't 'you know.'"

"Good, because that would be crazy."

"I know."

"Because everybody knows Reed isn't one to settle down."

"I know."

"And for all we know he may *never*—"

"I know."

"And then there's that Cravens wo—"

"I know."

"I mean, who knows what's going on with the two of th—"

"I know."

"And after all, Abby, Reed was Jason's best friend. This could ruin your—"

"I know. I know. I *know*." Abby stood and walked to the door. "Thanks for listening," she said dryly.

"Where are you going?"

"Home."

"What for?"

"To work on improving my vocabulary."

# Chapter Seven

"There's no hurry, Bill. Just wanted to make sure you've got the applicants lined up." The three-fifteen dismissal bell had barely rung and already Reed could hear the slamming of locker doors in the frenzied rush to get out of the building. He picked up the nameplate marked Principal and tapped it against his palm. "The foundation board meets next week, and you know how antsy Dad gets if you don't have a few names for them to toss around."

Bill Bates smiled from across his desk. "Yeah, between Ben and Miss Walsh, it's a tie as to who's more anxious. You'd think after all these years handling the Edith Mackintosh Scholarship, they'd both show a little more patience. It's only the second week of the term after all."

"Yes, well, Miss Walsh insists on tracking each candidate through the school year."

"Don't I know it," Bill said. "She makes these kids toe the line from the git-go. From high grades to sterling character. With a dose of community service thrown in for good measure."

"Right. The holistic approach according to Theodora Walsh."

Bill Bates nodded. "But you have to admit she's helped to relax the rules some. Remember the year you and I were seniors? One incident of bad conduct could get you tossed out of the running without so much as a hearing, thousands of dollars right out the window—although I noticed it never stopped *you*."

Reed smiled. "That's because I was never in the running."

"You know, I always thought that was a shame, too," Bill said. "You had the grades for it even if you didn't show up in class half the time. Hell, the scholarship was named after your mother, funded by your father and—"

"Do you begin to see a slight conflict of interest?"

Bill laughed and went to the door. "Maybe so. Let me see what's holding up those files."

Reed sat back in his chair and remembered the night he and Jason and Abby had celebrated Jason's winning the scholarship. Abby had been so proud....

Abby. To hell with back then. He needed to think about her in the here and now. He was trying hard to move slowly with her. It was clear she had some fears. Damn, so did he. She had passed him over once before for Jason. He couldn't stand the idea of Abby doing that again.

Still, he figured there was a chance of that very thing happening. She seemed so guarded at times. Perhaps she was having second thoughts about the move to Winston. He ached to get past that. Reed had always believed that Jason had in his own way been good to Abby. And good *for* her. Now that he knew the truth...

Bill Bates came back and handed over a few manila folders. "We'll have the others shortly, Reed. Is there a problem, Miss Hadley?" Reed looked up to see the aging school secretary standing in the doorway.

She nodded. "A brawl, I'm afraid."

"Another one?" Bill shook his head. "Who is it this time?"

"The same two as last week, Mr. Bates. John Crawford and the Malone boy."

The last name caught Reed's attention immediately. "Matthew? Is he—are they all right?"

"A few bruises coming up, some cracked knuckles, maybe a bloody nose, that's about it," she said as though after forty years in the school system she had seen it all and wasn't very impressed. "Coach collared them both and left them on the bench outside."

"Did Coach say what the ruckus was about?"

"A girl."

"Gee, that's a new one," Bill said dryly. "Thanks for letting me know. We'll let them cool their heels a little longer while I call their folks."

"Uh . . . could you hold up on that?" Reed said. "I don't want to tell you your business, Bill, but do you think we could talk about this . . . before you make the calls and get everybody in a tizzy?"

"Good Lord," Miss Hadley said. "Doesn't *this* bring back memories? Why, Reed Mackintosh, that's the same thing you used to say when you were a stu—" Miss Hadley cleared her throat and adjusted her glasses. "I'll just give the two of you time to discuss this," she muttered on her way out.

Bill Bates's eyes were chock-full of mischief. "So, what have you got to say for yourself this time, son?"

"Very funny," Reed said, but he would gladly take even more ribbing if it would help Matthew. Abby just didn't need this right now.

"Would you happen to be acquainted with either of these kids?" Bill asked.

As if he didn't know, Reed thought. As if the whole damn town didn't know. "I'm sure you're aware that Matt Malone is Jason's son."

"Yeah, I am." Now Bill's tone became more serious. "Are *you* aware that this is the third fight that boy's been in since school started?" He shook his head. "He sure doesn't come across like Jason did. To be honest, this boy sounds more like another kid I used to know...Mackintosh I think his name was."

"And maybe a bit like another kid we knew," Reed suggested. "Bates, I think his name was."

"Okay, okay, you've got me there," Bill said. "But Reed, rules are rules, and I'm bound to suspend the both of—"

"I have to admit Matt's gotten himself off to a rotten start, Bill, but I wish you'd reconsider. If not for him, then...hell, for old times' sake."

The principal spent a few seconds rubbing his jaw and then sighed. "I'll talk to them, but I'm not making any promises."

"Good. Thanks. All right if I sit in?"

"Okay with me. Sounds like you've got something in mind."

"I know Winston High doesn't have a boxing team anymore, but how about the equipment? Any of that left?"

"As far as I know, some of it's still in storage. Might take a few minutes to dig it up." Bill Bates went to the door again. "I see where you're headed with this, but let's have a look at the two of them first."

A definite sneer lifted one corner of Matthew's swollen mouth as he entered the office behind a red-haired boy who appeared to be right around his own weight and height. Heat and hostility ricocheted between the two of them.

"You two just stand over there by the window," Bill said as he went around the desk and took his chair again. "And we'll try to get to the bottom of this. You both know Mr. Mackintosh. He'd like to get to the bottom of this, too."

Reed almost laughed at the what's-it-to-you look Matt shot him before the boy faced front again. The damage to both teams was minor, Reed decided after a cursory glance at the messed-up hair and disheveled clothes. A little ragged around the edges maybe. Aside from the fat lip, Matt was sporting a trail of dried blood across his cheek. His opponent, John Crawford, a smart-mouthed transplant from over near Fayetteville, as Reed recalled, was coming on strong in the black-eye-and-bloody-lip department. It was clear Matt had rearranged a few of John's freckles. Both the boys' T-shirts were torn and blood splattered.

"Anybody want to tell me what's going on here?" Bill asked. As Reed had expected, there was total silence in the room except for the squeak of the principal's chair as he shifted. "All right," he said. "Let's start with the girl. What's her name, Crawford?"

John Crawford's Adam's apple went up and down as he swallowed once, and then he didn't move again.

Bill sighed. "The two of you should know that you're facing a two-week suspension for this. Somebody better start talking. Fast. The girl, Malone. Who is it?" he asked, and then waited.

Matthew drew in a breath. "Car—" He cleared his throat. "Carrie."

"Alexander?" Bill asked. "But I thought she was going with Frankie Benteen. Why would you two be fighting over her?"

Neither boy answered.

"Come on, guys. We're not kidding around here. Let's have it."

"Frankie didn't want to fight," John said.

"Well, gee, that's *dumb*. What do you suppose is *his* problem?" Bill Bates looked at Matthew. "So you fought John here, because Frankie wouldn't. Why?"

Again there was silence.

"What is this?" Bill wanted to know. "A power struggle to see which one of you is the biggest nitwit?"

"He . . . he said some things I didn't like," Matthew muttered.

"Oh," Bill said as if it made all the sense in the world. "He said some things you didn't like. And so you tried to whip the hell out of him."

"Well, I did my damnedest."

The kid had said it so simply, so honestly, that try as he might, Reed couldn't stop the certain pride that grabbed hold of his gut and swelled. Abby would kill him if she even suspected he was feeling this way. That's why Reed decided right then and there that it would be wiser to keep his pride to himself.

Bill got up and shoved his hands in his pockets. "Anybody feel like shaking hands and calling it quits?"

No one spoke.

"In that case, I guess you'll just have to shake hands and come out fighting. In the ring." He looked to Reed. "Right now a good time for you?"

"Fine by me," Reed said. "In the gym?"

Bill nodded.

Reed straightened the files in his hands and stood facing the boys. "Wash up and be in the gym in five minutes. I'll show you a few basics and then you can get right to it. Say three two-minute rounds with a sixty-second rest in between."

Matthew looked him square in the eye. "I don't want to fight."

"Fine," Reed said. "Then I take it you want to apologize?"

"No."

"Well, then?"

"You're gonna make us box?" the other kid asked. "Why can't we just settle it ourselves?"

"Oh, it'll be settled," Reed said. "You can depend on that. But the right way. With sparring gloves. You two can pound each other into the ground for all I care. Who knows, we might even sell tickets."

John Crawford's voice trembled some. "I'm supposed to be home right after school, ya know."

"Looks like you'll be late," Bill said. "Just be in the gym in five minutes. You hear? Five minutes."

Even with the mouthpiece and headgear, Abby knew it was Matthew sprawled faceup on the mat. After pushing her way through the crowd of screaming teenagers, she stood in stunned silence as her son struggled slowly back to his feet. So much for coming straight home before a dental appointment, she thought. He shook his head before raising his gloves and facing his opponent again.

"Way to go!" someone yelled. "Shake it off, Malone!"

Knowing only too well who that someone was, Abby swung her gaze to the opposite side of the ring where Reed leaned over the rope and called out some sort of instructions. To her son. Reed was letting her son do this. Even encouraging him to do this. Without a word to her.

Abby's head throbbed with the tension. There had been a lot of that lately. Matthew had been staying out later than she liked—always with one excuse or another—and hanging around with boys whose families she didn't know. And now this.

A loud smack to the jaw sent the red-haired boy staggering backward into the makeshift ropes. But Matthew didn't stop there. He advanced once more and swung a hard roundhouse, missing this time and giving the other boy a chance to regain his balance and get in a punch of his own.

Reed winced and put his hand to his forehead. "Aw, Matt! I told you not to loop your punches. Keep 'em straight, for God's sake."

It was then that she noticed the blood on Matthew's T-shirt. Abby went weak in the knees. She placed her feet more firmly on the floor and took several deep breaths.

"Crawford! Get your gloves up, you hear. Up!" Reed yelled. "Only half a minute to go. Malone, keep your elbows in and circle to the left."

Matthew did as he was told and received a light glancing blow to his forehead.

"No, no, *No!*" Reed cried out with an excited shake of his head. "Forget the face, Crawford! Go for the belly. Remember—kill the body and the head dies."

Abby's jaw went tight. The fact that Reed was giving another human being instructions on how to "kill" her son sent a righteous streak of anger through her. How dare he!

The other boy got in another good blow that seemed to stun Matthew for an instant before he came to his senses and became a moving target again. Voices from the old days— *Keep moving, Mackintosh! Punch straight ahead! Get your gloves up, stupid!*—mingled in her mind with the screams of the present for Matthew. She had heard them all before— the warnings, the encouragement, the jeers—and she had hated it then as she hated it now.

Then Matthew seemed to get comfortable in the ring. He began a series of combination punches—a left jab, a straight right, ending with a left hook to the stomach—that Abby had to admit were impressive for a beginner like Matthew.

The Crawford boy didn't recover enough to retaliate before some sort of bell clanged, reminding Abby a lot of the sound of a wooden spoon against the bottom of a saucepan. In any case, she realized the fight was finally over. Amid the cheering in the gym, Reed had already walked onto the mat and was looking a lot prouder than he had a right to, she noted, as he draped a towel over each boy's shoulder and kept right on giving instructions, probably an analysis of the entire match, too, if she knew Reed.

Matthew was breathing heavily. Sweat had poured off his face and made a wide dark circle around the neck of his T-shirt. The muscles in his arms had recently begun to bulk—at least she thought it was a recent development.

Now, as she watched him listening carefully, concentrating on whatever Reed was saying, Abby wasn't so sure exactly when her son's physique had begun to change. In any case, he looked beat as an excited Frankie pulled first one glove, then the other, off Matthew's fists.

The two opponents kept moving through the crowd, which eventually parted to clear a path to the showers. Matthew had his arm around the red-haired boy in a supportive hold. It was then that Abby saw the split lip, the bruised cheek. "Oh, my God," she gasped quietly as Matthew came closer.

Moving slowly past her, he kept his eyes straight ahead. "Mom, please don't," he whispered. "Just...don't."

Abby blinked back her tears and swallowed, forcing her hand to stay at her side. "See you at home," she whispered back.

"Okay, everybody," Reed called, "the show's over."

The group slowly dispersed and began moving out of the gym. Abby stood near the door and tried to get some perspective. But when the last student had left, no perspective had arrived.

Reed took his time picking up equipment, dragging the mat and the makeshift ring to one side of the room. When there didn't seem to be any more he could do to avoid her, Reed strolled over and smiled tentatively. "Hi, Abby."

"How in God's name could you let this happen? Without even trying to stop it?"

"Abby, it looks much worse than it is."

"My son is covered in blood. He's exhausted. He's hurt."

"He's fine. Just a little tired, that's all. It was either this or suspension. This is the third time in two weeks that he's been in a fight with this same kid. Skirmishes that really didn't settle whatever the problem is between them. I thought it was time both of them got it out of their systems once and for all."

"Oh, you did, did you? So this was all *your* idea."

"Yes, but Bill Bates agreed. You know, I have to give it to Matt. He's a scrapper, that one. They're pretty evenly matched in weight and height, but Matt seems to have a little more natural talent."

Abby tried to regain control of herself, but her voice trembled, as did her hands, which she curled into fists. "How dare you?"

"Abby, come on," Reed said. "It's not that bad."

She pushed his arm away and turned on him. "My son has been fighting like some Neanderthal, and you say that it's not that bad. Well, I think it *is* that bad, Reed. I think it's terrible. And I don't know how can you stand there and say it isn't."

"Abby, they're boys. They get mad. Sometimes they fight. That's how adolescents take care of their problems. One of the ways anyway."

"I thought we adults were supposed to help them get over that," she said. "I thought we were supposed to set standards. Give them other options. Obviously I was wrong."

"No, Abby, you weren't wrong. We *are* supposed to help them get over the urge to punch each other out."

"And yet you set up this boxing match."

"Yes."

"So that they could fight."

"Abby, they were *already* fighting. I—*we*—were trying to put an end to the fighting. Safely—well, with relative safety."

"And how did you hope to accomplish that?"

"Well, both of them look pretty spent to me. But otherwise unharmed. Maybe now they'll have to start talking. Who knows? They might even start thinking."

"Reed, I know you believe that boxing is an outstanding sport, that it promotes all kinds of self-esteem, confidence, that sort of thing, but—"

"Maybe. Maybe not. I think it helped me personally, but—"

"Well, I disagree," she stated flatly. "I always hated those matches that Jason dragged me to, just to watch you either beat someone up or be beaten to a pulp yourself. It killed me to see your face bruised and cut and—"

"Really?" He shrugged. "You never said anything."

"What good would it have done, Reed?" Abby realized that her voice had become louder. She took a deep breath and tried hard to maintain her composure. "Since when did you listen to me—or anyone else, for that matter? But it was what you wanted to do and Jason thought we should support you, so I went—"

"And I thought you just liked seeing me with my shirt off." He was smiling in such a maddening way. "In any case, I appreciated your being there."

"That isn't the point. I thought it was crazy and barbaric and—"

"Just the slightest bit exciting?"

"You're not going to take me seriously, are you?"

He sighed and looked away for a moment. Then he faced her again. There was no smile this time. "Abby, I know you don't understand. You've probably never been hit in the mouth by another person."

"Well, of course I haven't—"

"Well, at one time or another, most males do get hit in the mouth. Or the nose. Or the belly. Or maybe all three. It has to do with testosterone, I suppose. I don't know why that is. I only know it is. Even your precious Jason got into a fight once. It's best that boys know at least the fundamentals of self-defense."

"I suppose you're going to tell me it doesn't hurt."

"No. It hurts like hell. But it isn't the end of the world."

To her it was. Seeing Matthew bruised and bleeding *was* the end of the world. Watching someone hurt him. Again Abby shoved that painful vision aside.

"I understand, Reed. I simply don't agree. And since Matthew is my son, I hope that from now on you will do things my way."

"All right." Reed opened the wide metal door and let her pass in front of him. He followed her out into the sunshine and matched her pace as she walked toward her car. "But what if he comes to me and just wants to mess around with the boxing gloves, just him and yours truly? How would you feel about that?"

"I think I know my son, Reed. He won't."

"Look," he said, "if you're so certain, then you shouldn't have any qualms about letting him spar with me now and then—*if* he asks."

Abby thought about that for a moment. "If he does, then okay... but I'm betting he won't."

Reed in turn thought about *that.* "Hey, you're probably right," he finally said. "After all, as you said, he's your son, and I really don't have any right to interfere."

Damn right he didn't. At last he was ready to see reason. Abby slipped behind the wheel and switched on the ignition. Reed closed the door for her as she put the car in gear. She did appreciate his efforts with Matthew, even if she didn't agree with his methods. It seemed no matter how hard they tried, she and Reed were destined to misunderstand each other. And Abby wished it didn't have to be that way.

...

# Chapter Eight

Abby found Cinda in the conference room. Unfortunately, Reed and Ben were there, too. Abby kept her hand on the doorknob. "I didn't mean to interrupt. I'll come back when—"

"It's all right," Ben said. "Come in. You can help me make these two see reason."

Abby didn't like the sound of that. The three of them stared at her, Ben at the head of the long table, Reed and Cinda sitting on either side of him. "I'd rather come back later," she said. "I was told that Cinda was here, and I just assumed she'd be alone. I'll just come back."

Reed got up from his chair and came toward her. She hadn't seen him in days. Even though she was still smarting from the "Boxer Rebellion," as it had come to be known in her mind, Abby couldn't help noticing the nice fit of the light gray slacks he was wearing. The white knit shirt only emphasized the tan of his arms.

"We could use a fresh voice," he said. "Please. Stay." At close range, his eyes had a weary look about them. Slipping her hand from the doorknob, Reed led her around to his side of the table and gave her the chair next to his. "We've been discussing promotional ideas. For two hours we've been discussing that particular subject."

"And a damn dull subject it's become," Ben grumbled.

"Was there something you wanted to see me about?" Cinda asked.

Abby set down the file folder she'd been carrying, but she didn't let go of it. "Yes, but I'm afraid it's more of the same. A promotional idea—more an angle, actually, but it can wait."

"No need to wait," Ben said.

"Hell, yes," Reed said, rubbing his jaw. "If you've got something, by all means let's—"

"But shouldn't I go over it with Cinda first? If she approves, then she and I could work up some sort of presentation."

"Not necessary," Ben said. "Let's have it, Abby. Mrs. Cravens won't mind."

Even so, Abby looked at Cinda, thinking that the creative director ought to be the one to say whether or not she objected. The other woman gave a conciliatory—one might even say grateful—smile. "Of course, show us what you've got, Abby."

"Well..." She opened the folder and picked out the current fanfold list of employees she'd requested from Personnel. "I've been thinking what a rich heritage there is at Mackintosh in the way of furniture makers."

Ben looked a little confused. Reed looked more than a little tired. The lift of Cinda's eyebrows was coaxing, as if she was hoping for more than a mere statement of the obvious.

Abby hurried on. "I've spent the morning going over the list of employees just to update myself on changes, growth and so on since I left Winston. I noticed that you still have entire families working for you. In many cases, you have

second and third generation craftsmen making Mackintosh
home furnishings. There are even a few fourth generation
people...like you, Reed."

She could have sworn he was holding back a yawn. If the
three blank stares were any indication, she was definitely
losing her audience. "Look, have you ever considered pro-
ducing an industrial video that would showcase the *people*
at Mackintosh? Ben, since you seem hesitant to brag too
much about yourself or your company, how would you feel
about showing pride in your employees and their high level
of craftsmanship...?"

Ben got up to stretch and walked to the wide window of
the conference room. He was rolling up the still crisp sleeves
of his white shirt as though he was only just beginning to
work instead of having been at it for hours.

Late-morning sunlight played across the silver streaks in
his hair. He was still a very attractive man, Abby decided.
All six feet of him. Cinda had come to the same conclusion
judging by the hidden glances she sent his way now and then
when he wasn't looking.

Abby had noted the admiring looks a few times before,
but hardly knew what to make of them. As far as she could
tell, Ben had certainly done nothing to encourage such regard from Cinda. In fact, quite the opposite.

"Well, you've certainly given us a lot to chew on," Ben
said. "This idea of focusing on our people appeals to me. A
lot."

Abby sat back and gave up the floor for further discussion. When she had finally gotten her idea across, the response had been better than she had expected. Cinda had
immediately supported the "Mackintosh people at work"
idea. So had Ben. Even Reed was impressed. He'd asked
some pertinent questions and appeared to be satisfied with
her answers, at least those she could give on such short notice.

Ben was nodding thoughtfully. "We could use it across the board in our advertising. I'd like to have new brochures this year, an updated history of plant additions and so on."

"Yes," Cinda agreed, "I can see some very aggressive advertising and promotional programs coming out of this."

"I wouldn't want to call it 'aggressive,'" Ben said, which made it clear he didn't like Cinda calling it aggressive, either.

"Dad, I don't think she meant anything by it," Reed said patiently.

"Perhaps I should have said 'energetic,'" Cinda offered, fingering a strand of blond hair that had escaped the chignon at her nape. "In any case, I think you're right, Ben. This angle could work for us on several levels, from the ad slicks to the full-color statement stuffers that we offer our dealers."

There was a hint of excitement in the eyes Ben turned to Reed. "What do you think, son? Of Abby's video idea."

Reed's look was more cautious. "On the surface, I have to admit it sounds good."

"On the surface?" Ben challenged. "What the hell does that mean, on the surface?"

"Nothing, Dad. It doesn't mean anything...but the proposal needs a lot more thought than we've given it, obviously, and it will require some cooperation on the part of our key employees. That's all. As you said, it's a lot to chew on."

"Oh." Ben nodded and came back to the table. "Well, that makes sense. But right now I feel damn good about it. Abby, this video thing is...well, if it works out, it'll be a showstopper for sure. Just what we need for the major markets. I wonder if we could get it done in time to take it up north, maybe to Minneapolis...or what about Seattle?"

Abby shrugged uncertainly. After all, she'd only come up with the premise that morning.

"Dad, I would imagine a project like the one Abby's talking about would take time." Reed looked at Abby for confirmation.

"Well, of course it'll take time," Ben said. "That's why I think Abby should get started immediately."

"Er...wait a minute, please," Abby said, holding up one small, but she hoped not totally inadequate, index finger. "As I recall, you hired me primarily as an idea person, with a little copy writing here and there when you need it, and maybe some commercial design. *Print* design. Although I have to admit that following the progress of a video intrigues me, I'm afraid I don't know anything about making movies. I'd prefer to leave its production to the pros... like Cinda here."

Both men's heads turned toward their creative director. Abby wondered if either father or son had bothered to read Cinda's résumé. Abby had. That morning, she had come across it while going through the personnel files.

"She can do this with her eyes closed," Abby said, and before Ben's eyebrows could lift in doubt, she was reaching into the file again. "I think second place in an internationally known film festival is recommendation enough, don't you?" Abby set a copy of the résumé in front of each of the men. "I hope you don't mind, Cinda, but I thought they needed to know how right you are for this. Ben? Reed? The prize-winning video I mentioned was written, produced and directed by your creative director."

Reed gave Cinda an inquiring glance before he went to work on the first page and then quickly moved on to the second. Abby wasn't certain Ben was reading at all, although he kept his gaze trained on the résumé.

"What was the title of your...piece? Is that what you artistes call a movie?" Ben asked with rank skepticism. "And what was the subject matter?"

*"Caprice,"* Cinda said without a trace of apology. "A promotion for a new fragrance introduced by a cosmetic firm I once did some work for."

"Uh-huh," Ben said with a doubtful nod. "I really don't see what perfume's got to do with furniture..."

Abby resisted the strong urge to roll her eyes.

"...but I guess it'll have to do. After all, marketing is marketing, I suppose. How long will it take?"

"Offhand, I'd say a minimum of three to six months," Cinda said, "depending on how long it takes to prepare a script, get a camera crew togeth—"

"This isn't *Ben Hur,* for God's sake. Why so long?"

"I do have my other duties here at Mackintosh," Cinda said quite reasonably.

"Well, if this thing takes off the way I hope it does, we'll need you to ramrod the project," Ben said. "We'll have someone take up the slack in the marketing department."

As if anyone could do it, Abby thought.

"Yeah, the cleaning crew can take care of it on weekends," Reed said dryly.

"All right, all right," Ben grumbled, belatedly realizing how patronizing he sounded. "Maybe Abby here will agree to come in, mornings at least, and work with your staff. That is, if you're willing to do double—maybe even triple—duty for a while. Until the thing is done, that is, say... three months tops?"

Cinda's smile was gracious. "I'll do my best."

"You always do," Reed said, and Abby felt certain then that he had tremendous respect for Cinda Cravens. So did Abby, but she couldn't seem to shake the question of whether he felt anything else for the woman. He yawned once more and rubbed his eyes.

"Late night?" Abby asked.

"He's had a lot of those lately," Ben complained. "But I guess it's worth it if—"

Reed's warning stare cut Ben off. "It won't be much longer, Dad."

Abby opened her mouth and then closed it again. She had a suspicion she wasn't supposed to ask what wouldn't be much longer.

Cinda reached across the table to pat Reed's hand. "You really do look tired. Anything I can do?"

Reed shook his head. "Thanks, but I'll take care of it. You're welcome to come around for a progress report, though."

Nothing like being left totally in the dark, Abby thought. And she didn't notice him inviting *her* to come around for a progress report. Or anything else.

"A project at home," Reed offered in Abby's direction.

She didn't believe it for a minute.

"With the work load here and my, er, project at home, there isn't a lot of time for sleep these days," he said. "Or much of a social life, either."

Was he trying to apologize for not coming around lately? Reed seemed so centered these days, whereas Abby felt so scattered. "Here's hoping everything turns out to your satisfaction," she said, getting up from her chair. "Anyway, it's good seeing you so focused."

"Focused?" Ben said with a laugh. "Now that's something no one would have accused him of in the old days. Right, Abby? Mrs. Cravens, you won't believe this, but there was a time when this boy's life was so higgledy-piggledy that he couldn't finish a damn thing he started."

"Well, he seems to have made a complete recovery," Cinda said pleasantly.

"Yes, but not before he gave his old man several hundred of the gray hairs you see before you. Then there was his best friend, Jason—Abby's husband, you know—who followed through like you wouldn't believe. Set his sight on the Mackintosh scholarship and worked his rear off 'til he got it. Lord, how that boy could get things done. From the very beginning, he knew who he was and where he was going. There was none of this 'finding' himself. Not like the Ancient Mariner here," Ben said with a good-natured clap to Reed's back.

Abby swallowed her complete annoyance at yet another comparison between Reed and Jason. "It isn't as if Reed hasn't turned out to be a responsible, caring human be—"

"Oh, I know, I know," Ben said and then grinned. "Trouble is, for the longest time, Reed was still out there looking for that responsible, caring human being. In all the wrong places, I might add." He shook his head. "Some people have the damnedest time growing up. And then others—like Jason—just seem to be grown when they're born."

"No question about it," Reed said easily. "He was a good guy. And a good friend."

Abby's jaw had gone tight to keep her mouth from saying the words she so wanted to say to Ben Mackintosh. That Jason was not the person everyone had believed him to be. That Reed was not the person everyone had believed *him* to be. And that Ben should thank his lucky stars for the son he had.

"Well, enough of this," Ben said. "Son, we'd better move if we're going to make that lunch with the sales reps."

"Be right there," Reed said, touching Abby's arm to stop her from leaving the room with Ben and Cinda. "Will you be around this afternoon?"

"Oh, yes, I'll be here," she said more curtly than she meant to. "Molly's playing at a friend's house after lunch today, so I'll come back here for a while. But Reed, I just—"

"Abby," he soothed, "lighten up on Dad. He doesn't mean anything by it." His gentle stroke of her cheek helped ease her tenseness. Still, Abby wasn't about to let it go completely.

"I'll try," she said. But the irritation stayed with her all the way out to her car and during the drive to the elementary school. Throughout lunch with Molly and two other giggling five-year-olds, Abby was able to put it aside, giving in to it only at odd moments as she dropped off the girls and made her way back to Mackintosh.

At her work station, Abby sat down at the computer and called up the research she'd gathered so far on the employees. But every time she thought she had her ill humor in check, the feelings bubbled up again, eating away at her control until all at once she found herself knocking on Ben's office door.

"Open," he called.

Abby hesitated a moment, wondering what in the world she was doing, before she opened the door and went in. Ben's eyes were closed, his feet propped on the desk and his hands clasped behind his head. "Busy?" she asked, not knowing whether to sit or stand.

"Yeah," he said, rubbing one eyelid. "Busy napping." He put his feet on the floor and sat forward, straightening his tie. "What can I do for you?"

Now that she was facing him, Abby tried to figure out how to begin. She couldn't just light into the man. Ben was, after all, Reed's father. He was also an old and dear friend, and now her boss. Still, she wanted him to know how strongly she felt.

"Is something bothering you, Abby?"

"Yes. Yes, something is—has been—bothering me. For some time now." It seemed prudent to remain on her feet in case she needed a speedy exit. "It has to do with what you were saying to Reed this morning—and at other times, as well." Abby shrugged when no further explanation would come. "I don't understand why you do that to him."

"Oh?" Ben tugged on his ear and gave her a guarded frown. "I'm not sure I know what you're talking about."

"Why can't you just give him a little encouragement now and then instead of always reminding him of times when he wasn't exactly the greatest son on earth."

"Who says he wasn't the greatest son on earth?" he demanded gruffly.

"You do. At least you imply it. Every time you insist on bringing up the less-than-stellar incidents in his past. And then you bring Jason into it. . . ."

"Well, what did I say that was so bad?"

"Ben, Reed is not Jason. He never has been. He never will be. You're just going to have to accept that."

"Who says I want him to be Jason?"

"That's the message you give with your constant comparisons."

"What the hell are you talking about?" Ben demanded. He was getting angry. She was getting nowhere. But she could hardly back out now.

"Ben, I—"

"I think the world of that boy. You know that."

"I believe you do think the world of him," she said, standing her ground. "That's why it's so . . . confusing, the way you treat him sometimes. As if you don't want others to know how you feel about him. Or . . . as if you don't want others to know how good he is. Is that it?"

"No. I mean . . . I don't know . . . not exactly."

"Well, then what?" she asked softly. "What is it?"

Ben didn't say anything for several seconds. Maybe he was waiting for some sort of calm to return. She hoped that was it. Then he got up and moved to the venetian blinds, closed now to the activity going on outside his office. "I just don't want anybody to think that I see my son as . . . any more special than . . . anyone else's son." Ben gave the slightest shrug. "Although in a lot of ways, he's heads above any man in—well, you know what I mean, girl."

"But he *should* be special to you, Ben. He's your son. And he's a good son, too. True, he's made mistakes. Haven't we all? But hasn't he done enough penance?"

"Penance? I never meant to make him think he had to do penance. For *anything*. I had no idea it even bothered him for me to mention the stupid things he's done. Hell, I just think of all that as the hard lessons of life—although you have to admit Reed has taken the full curriculum in that schoo—''

"See what I mean?"

"All right. All right. Point taken, damn it. And as for the other, the comparisons, as you call them . . . I never meant anything by that, either. If he minded, he never said so."

"I know," she said. "For some reason, he hasn't wanted to confront you with this."

"So you're doing it for him."

Abby let out a breath. "Yes, I am."

The stare he turned on her was judgmental and intimidating. And long lasting. Abby stared back until he finally gave up and returned to his seat, putting his desk between them once more. "I've always tried hard to remember where I came from, Abby. I've tried hard to make sure Reed remembered, too. Maybe I've overdone it, been too critical with him. God knows my father overdid it with me."

Abby smiled. She'd heard stories.

"But I was crazy about him," Ben said. "And I respected him. In my own way, I guess I've been trying to pass on to Reed the things my father pounded into me. Like common decency. The ability to laugh at ourselves. And humility, Abigail. You know how I feel about anyone thinking we consider ourselves above anyone."

"I know. But I don't think there's any danger of that. I doubt even your worst enemies would ever call you arrogant. But Reed . . . well, Ben, he's your son. He needs to know that you're proud of him. That you think he's a decent human being with plenty of worth."

"Well, hell, of course I do," he said, waving her advice aside. "But he *knows* all that."

"I'm not sure he does. I think he wants to believe it, but he needs to be told now and then. He has such respect for you and, well, he loves you. And while we're at it," she said calmly, now that she appeared to be on a roll, "it's my opinion that Cinda also thinks highly of you. Although I could be wrong, the way you—"

"The way I what?" he challenged.

"Well, Ben, you're critical of her, too. And it seems to me that she does a wonderful job for your company, and she likes you so much."

"She does?"

"Yes."

"Then why doesn't she ever laugh around me? I swear that woman hardly ever cracks a smile."

"I've seen her smile lots of times," Abby said.

"Yeah, see? Maybe with you and other people, but with me... Hell, her face'd probably break."

"I think you make her nervous."

"The hell you say. I don't make people nervous. Just how do I make her nervous?" he demanded with a puzzled frown.

"Well...sometimes you get agitated. Like you are now."

"I am *not* agitated. I just like to get things done," he said. "I want them done well and in a timely fashion. Good God, is that too much to ask? What else?"

"What do you mean?"

"What else about me makes her nervous?"

"Well, maybe you expect too much out of her."

"I do not."

"Do, too," she returned crisply.

He grumbled something she couldn't make out and then more clearly, "Well, maybe it's because I know she can do most any job she tackles."

"Is that so? Then why do you convey the idea that you have zero confidence in her ability."

"I don't do that. Do I do that?"

Abby gave him a reproachful stare.

He cleared his throat and let out a deep breath. "It should be obvious to anyone with half a brain that the woman possesses talent."

"And?"

"Ability. She appears to have that, too."

"Oh? Maybe you should tell her that."

"Lord, Abby, why do I have to do that? Why can't I just tell Reed to give her a Christmas bonus like last year?"

"Because she'd like to hear it from you," Abby said. "Honestly, Ben, I think Cinda likes you."

"Aw, come on—"

"Sometimes I think she wishes you liked her more."

"You're kidding."

"No, Ben, I'm not kidding."

"Abby, I'm a country boy from Arkansas. With little education and sometimes even less good sense."

"That isn't true, Ben. And even if it were, what would it matter? I think Cinda has a great respect for you. But, look, I've said enough. I really came in here to talk about Reed and—"

"Well, ain't that a kick in the pants."

"Ain't *what* a kick in the pants?" she asked.

But Ben was already leaving the room. He stopped at the door and looked back. "You're sure about all this?"

"Well, of course I'm sure. Reed needs your support, Ben, and—"

"No, no, no. I know all that. I understand all that. I'll take care of it. I meant, are you sure about that other stuff?"

"What other—"

"Think she'd go out with me?"

"Who?"

"Cinda Cravens, that's who. Good God, stay with the conversation, girl." He closed the door behind him.

* * *

"Would you come into my office for a minute?"

He was peeved. She could tell. "Well, Reed, could it wait? I think I'm on to something here and—"

"Sorry, it can't wait," he said firmly. "I think we'd better make it now." Abby saved what she had so far on the computer, and got up from her chair. Reed set a brisk pace to his office, where he ushered her in and pushed the door closed. "What the hell is going on around here?"

"I don't know what you mean," she hedged.

"Dad came into my office—I thought the man was going to cry—telling me . . . well . . ."

"What, Reed? What was he telling you?"

"How much he loves me, for God's sake. Abby, my dad doesn't do that sort of thing. At least, he's never done it before. I thought maybe he was dying or something, wanted to square things with me before he . . . you know. What did you say to him, Abby? He got so upset that he was falling all over himself apologizing for . . . I don't even know what he was apologizing for."

"Well, did he mention that he was sorry he compared you with Jason?"

"No, he didn't mention that."

"Oh. Well, maybe he admitted he'd been too critical."

"No, he didn't say that, either."

"Then what *did* he say?"

Now Reed was scratching his head in the same way his father did. "He didn't get specific about anything. Just said he was sorry for the way he had treated me and he'd never make any more references to my past shenanigans if I didn't want him to. But damn it, Abby, that isn't the point. You're interfering in something that really isn't any of your business."

"Oh, I am, am I? Well, Reed, I'm sorry, but after this morning, I just couldn't sit by any longer without saying something."

"Abby, I'm a grown man. A grown man doesn't need parental approval."

"Why, that's nonsense. Of course you do. Everyone does." She wondered if there was some sort of gene marked "Hardhead" that the Mackintosh men passed along from one generation to the next.

"He doesn't owe me anything," Reed said flatly.

"He owes you respect," she argued. "After all, you turned out to be a fine man, and it's time he—"

"I did?"

"Of course you did. Don't you know that?"

"Well, at times I've thought so. Though I have to admit it's nice to hear someone else say it."

"And if you're honest, I think you'll admit that sometimes the things your father says about you bother you as much as they bother me."

Sliding his hands into the pockets of his pants, he thought about that for a minute. "No, not as much as they bother you," he said. "But yes, they do bother me a little."

"See?" she said, trying hard not to give way to the I-told-you-so smile that begged to spread itself across her face.

"I said a *little*." Reed came over to stand very close and looked down at her. She was surprised but thoroughly delighted when his arms went around her waist. "I guess I should thank you for your efforts on my behalf."

"No need," she said with cocky lift of her chin.

"Oh, yes, there's a need," he said. "A tremendous need. That is, after all, why I called you in here in the first place."

"Mmm-hmm. And here I thought you called me in here to berate, castigate and otherwise humiliate me."

"That, too. But then I was going to think of a way to show my undying devotion and gratitude."

"Oh. Well, in that case, a seven-course dinner will do."

"I was thinking of something more personal," he said. "And much more immediate."

The kiss he delivered was plenty of thanks and more, at least to Abby's way of thinking. She let her lips linger, thanking him for thanking her, and so on. They stayed in each other's arms for several long moments, presenting one another with small tokens of their esteem until Abby felt drugged with all the gratitude drifting back and forth between them.

She closed her eyes and sighed, leaning into him for physical as well as emotional support. Even though she knew that at that particular moment, anything more could only be an exercise in frustration, Abby couldn't help leading and letting herself be led right up to the edge of recklessness, where she was so tempted to let go of everything that was reasonable or wise. There seemed no place for reason when he nibbled her neck the way he was doing now. And wisdom was only a vague idea lost in the masculine thumb that teased her breast to a taut peak of excitement.

Reluctantly she pulled her mouth from his and let her hands slide from his neck down to his arms, but she didn't let go altogether. She closed her eyes and waited for her breathing to return to normal, which she suspected would've happened sooner were it not for the fact that Reed's finger was skimming along her lower lip in a slow and tantalizing trace of that particular feature.

"You should be ashamed of yourself, tempting a man like this," he whispered. "And in his place of business no less."

Wondering just which place of business he was referring to, Abby gave in to a smile. A small one. "So *this* is the thanks I get...."

"You could have more. A lot more, if you'd only accept it."

Abby said nothing. Mainly because she knew she wasn't ready for more.

His fingers fanned through her dark hair and swept it back from her face. "One of these days, we gotta stop meeting this way," he said.

"I know," she whispered. "What if Ben came in or—"

"That isn't the only reason."

She knew it wasn't.

"Abby, you're not . . . afraid of me. Are you?"

She was. But not of him, really. But of loving him. Of loving anyone again. Of trusting anyone again. But of him? "No," she said. "I'm not afraid of you, Reed. Look, I've got something cooking on the computer. I'd like to be able to show it to your father and Cinda this afternoon, so—"

"You know he's asked Cinda to have dinner with him tonight."

"What? But—"

"I think he's wanted to do that all along, but you know how stubborn Dad can be."

"Gee, I can't imagine what you're talking about," she teased. "And you don't mind his going out with Cinda?"

"Of course not. Why should I?" With a slow lift of her chin, he forced her to look at him. "Abby, surely you didn't think there's something going on between Cinda and me. Other than friendship, I mean."

"No. Of course not. Is there?"

"No. Abby, don't you know how much . . ." Reed looked away for a moment before facing her again with the most alluring smile. "Take my word for it. She'll enjoy Dad's company much more than mine. I think he really likes her."

"Yes, I'm beginning to understand that about your father. I guess he's one of those people who is most critical of those he really cares about. Add to that the fact that sometimes he feels a little inferior. Does that make sense?"

"Yes," he said, "as a matter of fact, it does. It made perfect sense the first time it occurred to me . . . about ten years ago."

"Oh. Then maybe I should've kept my mouth shut."

"On the contrary. If not for you, I doubt he'd be having dinner with Cinda tonight. And what you did on my behalf was sweet, Abby, and loving. Endearing, too."

Abby's mouth curved in affection. "Thanks. But I don't suppose I've endeared myself to your father, criticizing his relationship with you."

"Oh, I don't know. The last thing he said to me was 'I'll thank that girl to watch her smart mouth around the boss from now on.'"

"I see. Well, if our theory is correct, that probably means he's crazy about me."

"Indubitably."

"If not, then I hope he isn't one to hold a grudge."

"I have a feeling one evening with Cinda will make him forget all those nasty things you said."

She smiled patiently. "Do you suppose they'll talk about videos all evening?"

"I wouldn't care to speculate," he said and pulled her close again, making it very clear he didn't care to talk at all.

Thinking it best to get back to work, Abby left a light kiss on his chin and stepped out of his arms. "Maybe things'll be more relaxed between them now. I know Cinda will present him with an excellent video."

Abby smoothed her dress and moved to the door. Looking back at Reed, she weakened at the sight of a still-warm mouth, a manly jaw and a pair of very appreciative—and terribly sexy—green eyes returning her gaze.

"Are you disappointed that I don't know how to make movies?" she asked him.

"Absolutely not," he said in a deep whisper across the room. "It isn't movies I want to make with you."

"Oh."

# Chapter Nine

"Is this enough sanding?" Matthew held up the piece for inspection.

Reed ran his fingers over the smooth wood surface of the long notched cylinder that would form the shaft of the coat tree. "Almost there. Why don't you rest a few minutes, then go over it one more time," he said, going back to the chair he was staining at the other end of the long workbench.

Setting the piece aside, Matthew dusted his hands and hooked his feet on the side rungs of the tall stool he was sitting on. "Think Mom'll like it?"

"She'll be proud to have it in her entry hall," Reed said. "Anyone would. And I mean that, Matt."

The boy dipped his chin in modesty. "It isn't that hard. Sorta fun, sometimes."

Reed was glad to hear that. Matt had taken to wood like the proverbial duck to water. He was every bit as perceptive as Reed considered Ben to be. As exacting as he considered himself to be. The boy was a natural, if he'd ever seen one.

Dipping the tip of the brush into the stain, Reed gave the bristles a few smart taps against the rim of the can. "This time next year, you'll be designing your own pieces."

Matthew shrugged uncertainly. "Maybe. But there's a good chance we may be back in Little Rock by then."

"Oh? Why do you say that?"

"I got a plan. It isn't all worked out yet, but there's somebody in Little Rock—well, maybe he can do something that will get Mom to go back. If it goes like I want it to, we could be outta here by Christmas."

"Really." Reed was beginning to feel sick inside. Abby hadn't mentioned leaving anyone behind in Little Rock. "You seem awfully optimistic."

"You never know." But Matt sounded as if he knew very well. Reed didn't believe it. Wouldn't let himself believe it.

"Is this...someone your mother's close to?" he asked casually. "Someone special?"

"Special? To *Mom?*" Matthew asked with obvious surprise and disgust at such an idea. "Man, what are you talking about? Mom? You think my mom would ever fall in love...?"

"Okay, okay," Reed said quietly, injecting as much calm as he could into the words. "I wasn't accusing her of anything. But, Matt, you know, after a certain amount of time, your mother may meet someone and—"

"Not *my* mom," Matthew said with a very doubtful shake of his head. "She isn't like that, Reed. She just wouldn't do it."

"I see."

Reed went on silently staining the legs of the chair as he considered how best to get into the subject of his relationship with Abby. Discarding each possibility as it occurred, he finally decided he'd better not get into it at all. Not now. Not here. Some other time. Maybe when he had more guts. Or when he had hopes of a more positive, less hysterical response.

"Look, Matt, about this plan of yours—"

"Don't worry," the boy said sullenly, still apparently annoyed by any suggestion that his mother might be attracted to any man other than Jason. "It isn't anything illegal, if that's what you're thinking."

"Oh. Well, good . . . but, Matt, would it be so bad if you ended up staying here in Winston? If your plan doesn't work out, I mean. You've made some friends, haven't you?"

"Yeah, Frankie and a few others, but—"

"You're even getting to know some girls, aren't you?"

Matthew stiffened and then went to work doodling in the sawdust on the surface of workbench. "One or two."

"Well, then, would it be so bad?"

Matthew picked up the sandpaper and began sanding the shaft of the coat tree again. "I dunno," he said after a few seconds. "Sometimes, I think I might like it here, but then—" he shrugged "—I don't know."

He didn't seem to want to talk about the subject anymore. Reed finished up the chair and turned it upright before setting it aside to reach for another. Six down, four to go, he thought, a little tired from the late evenings. But he could honestly say he had enjoyed making the entire set. He took a few moments to carefully inspect the seventh chair for any nicks or rough edges he might have missed before wiping it down and reaching for the brush again.

"You'll be ready to stain your tree before long, Matt. As soon as you attach the base and hooks, that is."

"Yeah, Frankie wants to help with that."

"Speaking of Frankie . . . is he doing all right these days?"

"I guess so. Why?"

"No reason. It's only that the past few times he's been over here, he seemed distracted . . . as if there might be a problem."

"Oh," Matthew said with definite caution. "Well, his dad's been sick and Frankie's working lots of hours at the drugstore." The boy shrugged. "That's about all I know."

Judging from his sidelong glance in Reed's direction, something was going on.

"And Carrie," he said, taking a shot in the dark, "how is she doing?"

"How should I know? I mean ... okay, I guess."

"Still going out with Frankie?"

"Yep. Still is." Matthew held the piece of wood very close to his eyes as though inspecting it for termites.

"The three of you are lucky to be such good friends," Reed said.

"Yeah," Matthew replied with the slightest hint of regret. "We're good friends, all right."

"Of course, sometimes friendship can really get in the way ... I mean, if there's a problem—"

"There's no problem," Matthew said in the lightest of tones.

In other words, butt out, Reed thought. So he did.

It was almost six-thirty before Matthew finished cleaning up his workplace and reached for his backpack full of schoolbooks. Even though he had slung the pack over his shoulder and was headed toward the door, the going was slow, and Reed figured the boy had at least one more thing on his mind.

"Reed?"

"Yeah?" he said without putting down his brush.

"Did you ever have anyone special? I mean, a girl ... when you were my age. Someone you liked a lot?"

Reed hesitated, mainly because of who that someone had been. "Yes, Matt, I did. Someone I liked very much. Why do you ask?"

"No reason. Just wondering. Well, did you and she ever ... did you ... you know?"

Reed smiled to himself and went on working. "Not that it's any of your business but, no, we didn't 'you know.'"

"Oh. Well, any special reason?"

"Oh, yeah. A big reason. Her dad was about six-four and had a shotgun. That was the best reason I could think of. That and the fact that she was crazy about someone else."

"Oh. That makes it tough."

"Tell me about it," Reed agreed.

"Well, if you'd been the one she liked, do you think you would've...I mean, when you were my age—remember, I'm gonna be fifteen in five weeks—when you were my age, did you...?"

"I'd really rather not talk about my own personal experience, Matt. Mainly because I don't think it will help you much in any decision you might make, what with all the hazards you kids are facing these days."

"You mean STDs?"

"That's exactly what I mean. You know, Matt, part of being mature is knowing your limitations. Knowing when you're not ready for certain things and accepting that. Knowing how to enjoy all the stuff that you *are* ready for and saving the rest for later when you'll appreciate them a lot more."

Matthew sighed heavily. "Yeah, I guess that makes sense. If only..."

"Yeah," Reed agreed with a smile, "if only."

"I was going to see somebody tonight, but she—I mean they—well, maybe I won't. Maybe I'll just hang out or maybe rent a movie."

"Good thinking. You're probably better off concentrating on movies and school and other things like sports right now."

"Hey, I've been meaning to ask you. Do you think you and I could spar with the gloves sometimes, if you have time, I mean?"

"Sure. No problem," Reed said, wiping his hands on a shop cloth. "What about this weekend? Just be sure and tell your mother what you have in mind."

It was clear by the look on his face that the kid had been hoping for secrecy. "Okay, but she'll probably give me some grief."

"Maybe not. I'm betting she won't. In any case, it's always best to be up front with these things," he said with more wicked satisfaction than he had felt in a long time.

"Okay," Matthew said doubtfully, and then he opened the door. But he still didn't leave. "About that other stuff, I hope you won't mention to Mom that I said anything about you know. I don't think she really understands about guys and stuff. I mean, how they feel and everything. She doesn't really know what's going on in my head these days."

"Is that so?" Reed shrugged. "You could be right, I suppose. But Matt, you shouldn't underestimate your mother. She may understand a lot more than you realize. Maybe she does know what's going on in your head."

"You think?"

Reed hid a smile as he watched Matthew's face turn a bright red.

"Oh, jeez, I hope not."

## *Chapter Ten*

"Can I open my eyes yet?"

"No!" Molly squealed, holding on even tighter to Abby's hand. "You'll spoil *everything,* Mommy."

"Yeah, Mom," Matthew said from Abby's other side, "keep those baby blues closed until we tell you to open them. We'll go slow, so you don't trip on the rug or anything."

Abby did as she was told and let herself be led faster than she liked toward the great room. "Mother, can you close the door?" she asked over her shoulder. "As you can see, I am otherwise occupied."

"Absolutely," Ellen Lindstrom said. "And I've put your purse and packages on the deacon's bench."

"Thanks. Just give me a minute and I'll put them a—"

"Surprise!"

The several voices calling out in unison opened Abby's eyes to a roomful of people, all laughing and wishing her well. Becky and Tom, Reed, Ben and Cinda and Charlie Johnson were only a few of the familiar, welcome faces. Her father stood beside Henrietta Walsh, who was hard to miss with a big red bow crowning her head, while Theodora stood in stark contrast, lips pursed, hands clasped together in unfailing dignity.

"What a nice surprise" was all that Abby could get out before her daughter pulled her farther into the room.

"Look what we did," Molly said, still bouncing up and down. "And I helped!"

"And you did such a great job," Abby said, looking past the smiles to the hearth, where the words Happy Birthday formed a very impressive silver arc above the fireplace.

She bent low for a kiss from Molly, and then the little girl was off and running to the punch bowl set up near the bay window. Even Matthew managed to drop a brief kiss on his mother's cheek with only a little embarrassment before he, too, made his way to one of several platters of finger food situated at strategic points around the room.

Joe Lindstrom was the first to collect a hug. "Happy birthday, Abigail."

"Thanks," she said, standing on tiptoes to wrap her arms around her father's neck. "Are you and Mom responsible for this?"

"Nope. Rebecca Wayne got it all together. As you now know, your mother was designated to keep the birthday girl busy, and I, well, I just showed up for the champagne," he teased. "All in all, not a bad way to spend a Saturday afternoon."

"Not a bad way at all, Dad. Guess I'd better mingle, huh? Take care of my guests and all that."

"Oh, no, you don't," Becky said, coming to her side, "Tom and I have everything under control. Your job is to sit in that chair—" she pointed to Abby's favorite rocker "—and hold court. After all, a person your age needs lots of rest."

"Need I point out that you, too, are a person my age?" Abby quipped.

"You could, but it wouldn't be wise, considering that I know where your gifts are hidden."

"I'll keep that in mind," Abby said, giving Becky's arm an affectionate squeeze. "Thanks for... all this."

Becky swept her red hair to one side and waved away the gratitude. "It's nothing. By the way, I told Molly and Matthew that they could each invite someone to your party. Molly, of course, chose Reed. Like mother, like daughter, I guess."

Abby smiled. "What about Matthew?"

"He never actually told me. Uh-oh, gotta go. I see someone with an empty glass," Becky said and was gone, leaving Abby to scan the room for Frankie or possibly Carrie Alexander, the two most likely people on Matthew's list of possibilities.

Abby could feel Reed's presence behind her. She turned and was promptly greeted with a glass of wine, which he pressed cordially into her hand. Then he leaned very close to deliver his own brand of birthday salutations. His lips touched her cheek, suffusing her face with a pleasant tingle. He pulled back slightly, leaving behind a wake of tantalizing warmth.

At that moment, she would have traded several birthdays for just a few minutes alone with him, to feel his arms around her, his mouth tasting hers, his hands moving over her. However, with the Walsh sisters looking on, both primly clutching their purses, Abby made do with a deep breath and a smile.

"Let's ditch these guys and go to the river," Reed whispered, sending the mildest shiver across her shoulders. "I'd kill for another look at those luscious thighs."

"Will you look at that, Dori?" Henrietta said. "I do believe Abby's blushing. Reed Mackintosh, are you threatening to tell everyone how old she is?"

"That's it," Abby lied. "That's it exactly. And after he promised he wouldn't."

"Nonsense," Theodora said. "If nothing else, Mr. Mackintosh is a man of honor."

"Thank you, Miss Walsh," he said, openly astonished that this particular woman would pay him a compliment. "Your defense is very much appreciated."

"If totally undeserved," Abby murmured softly, trying hard not to respond to the masculine hand teasing the small of her back.

"All right, everyone," her father said. "Choose your poison—punch or champagne—and get ready to toast the birthday girl."

"You ladies seem to have been caught without libation," Reed said to the Walsh sisters. "May I get you something?"

"Well," Theodora said uncertainly, "we don't usually drink alcoholic bev—"

"Nonetheless," Henrietta interrupted, "on certain occasions we do adore a good white wine."

"Not that we would ever overindulge," Theodora said quickly.

"Mercy, no," Henrietta said with a shake of her head.

"Well?" Tom asked, a bottle of wine poised above two empty glasses. "Is that a yes or a no? Is Abby's birthday special enough or would you rather—"

"Oh, heavens, yes," Henrietta said. "We'd enjoy a tiny sip, wouldn't we, Dori?"

"Of course. It would be impolite not to toast Abigail's special day."

As soon as the drinks were served all around, Joe Lindstrom put his arm around his wife and raised his glass high. "Now, folks, Ellen is going to help me with this because she is, after all, the one who made this possible to begin with. Thirty-six years ago today, this lovely—not to mention tired—lady finally gave birth to..."

Hardly hearing the words, Abby was caught up in the scene of her mother's face at rest against her father's chest.

After all these years, there was still unmistakable regard in the work-worn fingers stroking Ellen's softly graying hair. Abby felt a pang of longing. She wanted for herself what the two of them had together. Had always had as long as Abby could remember. The strength, the respect and trust. The comfort. A marriage that had survived and thrived through everything life had thrown at it.

Was it even possible for her at this late date? With Reed? With anyone? She glanced up at Reed and found that he was looking back at her.

"Here's to you," he whispered, "and to us," she thought she heard him add before he joined the others in drinking to her health. Surrounded by friends, Abby felt her heart slowly filling with hope. "I've asked Becky to hold off on the cake and candles until I can show you my gift," he said.

"Gift? Reed, you didn't have to."

"Oh, but I did." He took her glass and set it aside before reaching for her hand again. "It's in the dining room."

"Oh, dear," Henrietta said as Abby prepared to follow his lead through the small crowd. "I do hope he doesn't give her the same kind of bows that he gave me for my birthday."

"I wouldn't fret about it," Theodora said dryly.

"So," Abby whispered, once she and Reed were alone in the hallway, "you're the one responsible for Henrietta's interesting headgear of late."

"Yep. I bought her one gewgaw for every day of the week. Nice and big and bright, every one of them," he said, moving Abby along toward the dining room. "They give her a little more height so I can spot her when she creeps along the fence to spy on me in my backyard." Reed halted Abby at the doorway. "Are you ready?"

"Do I have to shut my eyes for this?" Abby asked with a bemused smile.

"I don't think that'll be necessary."

The parting of the tall wooden doors brought an instant gasp from Abby. "Reed! A table? You're giving me a dining table? And matching chairs." And so *many* matching chairs.

Reed switched on the chandelier and the soft light danced across the rich dark oak finish. "Happy birthday again," he said. "I wasn't sure I could finish everything in time, but—"

"You made this? You did this for me?"

"Especially for you, Abby."

"Country Irish. Oh, Reed, it's my favorite."

Abby couldn't resist running her palm along the gleaming tabletop. She bent down to examine the beautifully carved stretcher between the scrolled legs. There on the inside of the frieze she found the small round metal stamp that bore the Mackintosh insignia along with Reed's name in Gaelic. An undeniable lump formed in her throat.

The glow of the wood, the curve of the legs, the insignia—all blurred through the tears she was fighting. There was no use denying any longer the love she felt for him. Even if he saw it as a birthday gift, a simple gesture of friendship, Abby saw it as so much more.

"It's . . . too much," Abby said shakily. "It's simply too much." He had closed the doors behind them, giving the two of them relative privacy. Abby was glad of that because she very much needed to slide her hands up around his neck and somehow show her feelings. "It looks perfect in here," she said. "But then it would be perfect anywhere. I'll cherish it, Reed."

"I know you will," he said, looking down at her. His eyes took on a teasing gleam. "You wouldn't be angling for a matching buffet at Christmas now, would you?"

Abby smiled, at once excited and uncertain of just how deep his own feelings ran. Her heart ached for enlightenment. With that aim in mind, she reached up to kiss him, letting her lips convey the emotion she felt. With the lightest of moans, he returned the good tidings, aligning his body to hers, insinuating an ever-growing need for whatever she was willing to give.

The door slid open slightly, but no one appeared. "Hey, you two," Becky whispered from the other side, "people are beginning to ask about the sudden disappearance of a certain birthday girl. Maybe you'd better get back to the party before folks begin to draw the wrong conclusions."

"Or worse still, the right ones," Reed said with a sigh.

Abby smiled her amusement. "Maybe we'd better go."

"Later?" he asked, refusing to release her until she promised.

"Most definitely," Abby said, and kissed him once more before leading him down the hallway, where Matthew was huddled in the corner with the telephone. His back was to her, and Abby sensed her son's agitation.

"Look, man, don't be mad," he was saying to someone on the other end of the line. "I know she's your—hey, this is stupid, and I—" He stopped in midsentence when Abby touched his arm.

"Who is that, Matthew?" she asked.

"Nobody," the boy muttered.

"I said who is it, son? Is there a problem?"

"Frankie," he said irritably. "And no, there's no problem, Mom. Jeez, can't a guy have a conversation without his mother listening in and giving him the third degree?"

"A guy certainly can," she told him firmly. "If a guy knows how to go about it in a civilized way and show a little respect. Otherwise, a guy can get off the phone and go to his room. Do you read me?"

"Loud and clear," Matthew said with a sigh. "Sorry, Mom."

That was better, she decided. Much better. She would have said more except that Reed was pulling her away again. "What do you suppose that was all about?" she asked him.

"I really couldn't say," Reed said with a shrug.

Couldn't or *wouldn't,* Abby wondered.

"But I do know that everyone's waiting to sing a certain song to you," he said, ignoring the skepticism emanating from her eyes.

And then the doorbell rang.

The tension in his shoulders relaxed as Abby went to answer it. She opened the door to a good-size man who was wearing a well-tailored suit and a damnably pleasant smile. Reed would also have to say he might be considered handsome in an older, graying-at-the-temples sort of way.

"Douglas!" she said, and immediately stepped forward to hug the guy.

Who the hell was Douglas? Reed wondered. And who invited him to this celebration?

"How good to see you," Abby was saying. "Come in." She was literally pulling the man inside the house, and then she was closing the door. "You're just in time for the party. It's my birthday, you know."

"You don't say," this Douglas person said. "Then isn't it lucky I brought this along?" he asked, reaching into his pocket to produce what Reed thought was a pitifully small package.

"Why, Douglas," Abby said, "you didn't have to bring me anything." Then she gave Douglas what was, Reed suspected, her most charming smile. "But as long as you did, shall I open it now?"

"Of course," the man said.

She tore into the package like nobody's business, Reed observed sourly. Finally, she noticed him. "Oh. Reed, this is Douglas Canfield. *Dr.* Douglas Canfield, I should say. Jason's medical partner," she explained with the merest glance at Reed. "Douglas, meet Reed Mackintosh. He's my—"

She stopped tearing the paper long enough to look up once more. This time she gave Reed a good hard stare. A thoughtful one. As if she was deciding for the first time just what he *was* to her. And then she gave him a smile, one that fairly melted any jealousy or hard feelings he might have been harboring.

"I'd say Reed is my best friend," she said quietly. And so easily that Reed saw no good reason not to offer the man a welcome hand.

"Pleased to meet you, Dr. Canfield."

"Please, call me Douglas."

"Oh, look. A miniature picture frame," Abby said.

"Hand carved," Douglas added.

Good, Reed thought. Inexpensive. Impersonal. Hell, one might even say generic. A gift he could have picked up at any roadside shop between Winston and Little Rock. Good, he thought again.

"How thoughtful," Abby said. "Thank you so much, Douglas. I'm so glad you're finally paying us a visit."

"I could hardly miss your birthday," he said.

Abby looked at him curiously. "But how did you know?"

"A certain young man—one who apparently thinks a lot of you—called last week to remind me."

"Oh," Abby said with a slow nod.

"Sure," Matthew said. Coming up from behind his mother, he stepped between her and Reed. "When Becky said I should invite someone to the party, I knew you'd want Dr. Canfield to come."

"Oh," Abby said again. "That was very sweet. Then I guess I should thank you, son."

"Yeah, that's our Matt," Reed said. "Always thinking of others."

"Right," Abby agreed uncertainly. "Well, Douglas, come in and meet everyone. We'll be cutting the cake soon."

"I can't stay long," Douglas said, moving alongside Abby. "I've got to be back in time for rounds this evening. You remember those, I expect. But I was hoping to get a few minutes with you before I go."

"Of course," she said, leading the way. "But first I want you to meet my parents. It's too bad that Jason's mother and dad won't be back from Florida until next week sometime. I know they'll be disappointed to have missed you, but..."

"Wait just a minute there," Reed said, tapping Matthew's shoulder when the boy started to follow Abby and the good doctor. "Is this the plan you were telling me about? To get your mother back to Little Rock?"

"Yeah," Matthew said, turning with a confident nod. "And you know what? I think it just might work. I mean, she was really glad to see Dr. Canfield. Did you notice that? You know, that guy's spent more time with me than my own d—" He stopped short, flipping dark hair the color of Abby's out of his eyes. "Anyway, she always listens to him. At least, she always has before."

Reed felt sorry, really sorry, for the kid. "Matt, listening is one thing. But going along with what he says—or what you want—may be something else entirely."

"Well," Matthew said with a shrug, "I gotta try, don't I? Hey, Mom's going to open her presents, and I want to be there when she sees the coat tree."

"All right," Reed said. "Look, about this thing between you and Frankie—"

"There's nothin' goin' on with Frankie. Everything's cool."

Reed stared at the floor. If only Matt had been his son— his and Abby's. Surely they would have been able to talk to each other better and— He shoved the thought aside and went back to the party.

"Do you know what it is?" Molly asked.

Reed shifted the little girl on his lap for a better view of the design she had made with beans for her mother's birthday. "Well, I think it's coming to me," he said, wondering if he shouldn't just give up and tell Molly the truth. He had already turned the sheet of construction paper this way and that and still couldn't figure it out. "But you know," he said, flicking a crumb of the birthday cake from her chin, "I'm really not sure yet."

Abby should be here, he thought, to help him in his time of need. But she was still holed up in the TV room with *Dr. Canfield.*

"You don't know what it is, do you?" Molly teased, looking awfully proud that she knew something he didn't.

"No, I'm sorry, I don't. But I'll sing 'Sweet Molly Malone' three more times if you promise not to be mad at me."

"Why, it's *beans,* silly. Lima beans, pinto beans and red beans."

"Oh," he said with a nod, wondering if he still had to sing.

"Dried, of course," she added.

"Of course. Wet beans would really be messy. But the shape...what's it supposed to *be?*"

"How should I know?" she answered with a shrug. "Just some dumb ol' design, that's all."

"Oh. Well, I'm glad we've cleared this up," Reed said, glancing over at Becky, who was doing an incredible job keeping the guests occupied in Abby's absence.

"Julianne's mother taught me how to do it," Molly said. "She makes lots and lots of stuff with beans."

"Does she now?" Reed said, thinking that Julianne's mother ought to find something better to do with her time. And her beans.

"Julianne's mother knows how to do all kinds of things," Molly said, and then sighed her disappointment. "My mom isn't very good at stuff like this."

"Well, maybe not with beans," Reed defended quietly, "but, Molly, your mother is smart in so many other ways. However, she doesn't do things to excess."

"Does Julianne's mother do things to ess...ess-ex?"

"Most assuredly."

"Well," Molly said, still clutching the picture as she slid down from his lap, "I'm just going to tell Mommy to keep working *very* hard, and pretty soon I bet she'll be able to do things to essex, too."

Molly walked over to discuss the whole thing with Henrietta Walsh, who probably knew more about beans than Reed did.

The door across the hall opened and Reed got up and went over to stand at the fireplace. Abby came out of the den and smiled at him. But there was a hint of worry in her smile. Douglas Canfield followed her congenially into the great room. She took stock of the remaining guests—Tom, Henrietta, Ben and Cinda, her parents—and then moved toward Reed. Just before she reached him, Matthew stepped into her path.

"Well," he said, "what do you think, Mom? Did Dr. Canfield convince you?"

Abby laughed and took a sip of wine. "I'm afraid not, son, but it was a nice try. I'm really glad you talked him into coming for a visit, but next time maybe you should check with me about motives."

"But, Mom—"

"Matthew, let's talk about this later. We do have guests, you know." She patted his shoulder and walked to the fireplace to stand beside Reed.

"Did you even listen to what he had to say?" the boy demanded.

Reed could see trouble coming. "Matt, maybe you and I should go for a walk."

"I don't want to go for a walk. Did you *listen?*" he asked his mother again.

"Of course I did," Abby said. "But, Matthew, we're settled here now. I wouldn't even consider moving again. I have a job here and—"

"Yeah, but didn't he offer you a job as office manager in the clinic?"

"I couldn't possibly accept it," Abby said. Her voice had become soft and low, tinged with bitterness. But she rallied admirably and smiled again. "As I told Douglas, there are many things I wouldn't want to go back to in Little Rock."

"To tell you the truth, I can't imagine why you'd want to go back, either," Douglas told Matthew. "Your mother tells me you've made friends here. Your family's here. And Winston looks like an awfully nice place to me."

"We think it is," Ben said easily. "I've been to a lot of places in my time, and I'd take this town over Little Rock any day."

"Yeah?" Matthew said testily. "Well, maybe you don't know everything."

"Matthew!" Abby said in breathless warning.

"Look, son, I didn't mean anything by it," Ben said with a shrug. "It's only that—"

"Maybe you just ought to mind your own business," the boy said.

"Matthew, stop it this instant!"

"And let *us* decide where we wanna live. You're just an old guy who's lived here for a hundred years, but that doesn't—"

Reed clamped a hand on Matthew's shoulder and boosted him toward the door. "Son, let's talk."

Moving the boy past Henrietta's gaping mouth, Reed provided strong encouragement for Matthew to move out the door to the end of the hallway, where he promptly pushed the boy up against the nearest kitchen wall and held him by the sheer force of his angry gaze. "You ever say anything like that again," Reed said, "and you'll be one sorry young man. Do you understand?"

"Wha-what'd I—"

"Do you *understand?*" Reed asked again. Matthew was breathing heavily as though he might be a little scared. Reed hoped he was a lot scared.

"Yeah. I understand."

"Good. That man is a decent human being who's been nothing but good to you and your family. More importantly, he's somebody's father. *My* father."

"I know who he is," Matthew said quietly.

"Do you really? Well, then know this, too. Not you or anyone else is going to talk to him the way you just did and get away with it. Got it?"

Matthew said nothing for a moment. Then he swallowed hard. "I got it," he murmured.

"And another thing," Reed said. "I understand that you're disappointed. And bitter. And mad as hell. I'm just beginning to understand why and what this is really all about. But kid, you're going to have to accept the fact that you'll be living here in Winston. At least for a while. And you've got to learn that if you want to get along in this town or anywhere else, you'd better get that chip off your shoulder. But then you don't want to get along, do you? I don't think you give a damn about—"

"Reed, what on earth . . . ?" Abby stood in the doorway. "What's going *on* in here?"

It was then that Reed realized just how angry he was. And how very much he had wanted to make things work with this kid. How much he had wanted to get through to him.

Abby took one look at her son's pale face and wanted to go to him. But she didn't go. She saw Reed's anger and couldn't seem to go to him, either. The man and the boy stared at each other for long moments until finally Matthew broke eye contact and brushed past her, leaving the room in an electric silence.

His footsteps on the stairs echoed the pounding of her heart. She had never handled her children in the way that she had just witnessed Reed handling her son. The very idea left her struggling with the tears threatening her eyes. And to think that anyone—even Reed—could speak to her child with such anger... Abby turned away, unable to accept that.

"Abby."

His hands touched her shoulders, but she pulled away. "Reed, I understand that Matthew was wrong. But did you have to treat him like that? Like he's some sort of— Did you have to shove him and..." Abby touched her mouth briefly to stop its trembling before she faced Reed again. "I'm sorry for what he—"

"Don't apologize for him, Abby. Please. You've got to stop apologizing for his rudeness, his insolence. Put the responsibility for his actions where it belongs. On *his* shoulders. Or else you're going to have a bigger problem than you know on your hands."

"Maybe. But I can't stand the idea of treating him so roughly."

"Okay," Reed said with a lift of his hand. "Then how would you have handled it?"

"I guess I would have talked to him."

"Talked to him?"

"Yes," she said defensively.

"Tell me something, Abby. How many times have you talked to him about this sort of thing?"

She couldn't count the times. And so she said nothing.

"That's what I thought." Reed ran a weary hand through his hair. "Abby, don't you see that if this doesn't stop soon, he will have blown any chance of fitting in here in Winston?"

"I know that."

"The kid makes no effort."

She knew that, too.

"He won't *let* people like him. At least not very many."

"I know. I know. I *know*," she said impatiently. "But I just don't believe that violence is the best—"

"*Violence?*" he asked. "You call what I did violent? Abby, I'm trying to prevent some real trouble. The kind that boy is going to run up against if he doesn't grow up very soon."

"You're getting angry again," she observed.

"Yes," he said, nodding vigorously, "I am getting angry again. Every time I think about the things Matt said. To my father..."

"Reed, I know it hurt you."

"Yes, it did. Because...he's my dad, for God's sake, but even more than that, maybe it just took me back to a time—maybe I'm just feeling guilty and ashamed for all the hell *I* must have put the man through." Reed shook his head bitterly. "God, I must have been such a disappointment."

"Reed, that isn't tr—"

"Anyway, I think I'd better go. And I'm sorry that I handled this whole thing in a way that's...unacceptable to you."

"Oh, Reed, don't. It isn't that—"

"Look, it's your birthday. I wanted to take you someplace special for dinner, but..." Reed came very close, his eyes pleading for understanding. He touched her arms only briefly before he held his hands away and stepped back. "Some other time, okay?"

"All right," she whispered, not knowing what more to say. The door closed softly behind him.

Abby sat down at the kitchen table and rested her face in her hands. He was right, she decided. Reed had been absolutely right. And although she didn't truly understand the intensity of his anger, she knew that he was basically a fair and just man. A good man. But so was Matthew. Despite everything he had done and said, despite his anger, his insolence...her son was a good son. She knew that as well as she knew anything.

"Abby dear?"

She looked up and saw a very ill-at-ease Theodora holding a half-full glass of wine as she stood in the doorway of the room just off the kitchen. "Miss Walsh. I didn't realize you—"

Theodora nodded uncomfortably. "Yes, well, I certainly didn't mean to eavesdrop, but I was admiring your bego-

nias, and when . . . *things* began to happen, there seemed no
way for me to remove myself. Nothing like getting between
a rock and a hard place, is there?''

"It's all right," Abby said. "I'm only sorry that you were
forced to hear all of the terrible—"

"Oh, goodness gracious, think nothing of it. Happens all
the time with teenagers."

"It does?"

"My, yes. Not with you, of course. You were always such
a sweet child, but you simply must keep things in perspective, Abby dear. I, myself, find that every now and then one
of these—" Theodora indicated her glass of wine "—helps
immensely with this sort of thing. Perspective, I mean."
Abby was instantly charmed. Theodora patted the silver-
streaked bun at her nape and pulled out a chair. "May I?"

"Of course," Abby said, knowing Becky would take full
charge of the party on her behalf.

"He's a good man, you know. That Reed Mackintosh."

"He'd be pleased to hear you say that."

"Oh, he was a dreadful tease in school and—"

"Still is," Abby whispered.

"—he did ruin my prize roses with that ridiculous motorcycle." Theodora took one last sip of wine and touched
a finger to each corner of her mouth. "But basically, he's a
decent human being, I suppose."

"Oh, yes," Abby agreed. "It's taken some time, but over
the years, I'm sure lots of people have learned that Reed
isn't quite the hooligan everyone thought he was."

"Oh, I knew it a long time ago. While he was still in high
school, actually. In fact, I knew it the very day he brought
that bus back from Tennessee."

Abby wondered just how many glasses of wine Miss
Walsh had enjoyed so far that afternoon. "I shouldn't think
that particular incident could be called one of his finer moments."

Theodora smiled, pursing her lips and rotating the stem of her now-empty glass on the tabletop. "That's because you don't know what really happened. Considering how that boy loved you and Jason . . . well, you're probably the last person he would have told."

"Oh, really," Abby said, positively burning with curiosity. "Then why don't you be a dear and tell me yourself?"

# Chapter Eleven

"Why didn't you tell me, Reed?"

"Because there was no point in it," he said a bit crossly. "I don't know why she even mentioned it. What does Theodora Walsh know about it anyway?"

"She knows that when the bus pulled onto her street at dawn that morning, Jason was the one who was driving. She was certain of it. So why don't you tell me how that came to be, when you were the one the sheriff arrested for stealing the team bus?"

She said this all very quietly, low-key, a sad kind of anger and regret burning her throat as she waited. Reed appeared to be ignoring both her concern and her request for an explanation, concentrating awfully hard on wrapping a simple cord around a simple jigsaw. And he took his own sweet time returning it to its place on the shelf.

"Reed?"

He looked up. "You know, I'm hungry," he said. "It's been a long day with your birthday and all. Aren't you hungry?"

"No, I'm not."

"What about the kids?"

"Becky's feeding them fried chicken."

"Oh. Well, you've got to eat something. Could I interest you in some pasta?"

"You could interest me in some truth. Consider it another birthday present. Reed, I want to know."

He gave her a skeptical glance and went back to his workbench. "You're not going to leave me alone about this, are you?"

She stared, a resolute look in her eye.

He let out a breath. "All right. It's really very simple. Jason got hold of some beer the night before the championship in Jackson. He drank until the wee hours. The next morning, I left him in the hotel room to sleep it off."

"But...Jason didn't even like beer."

Again with the skepticism. "He liked it well enough that weekend, take my word for it. Anyway, just before my match that day, I went out to the bus for my gym bag. He was there alone, dangling the keys and giggling. Said he had stolen the keys while the driver was snoozing, and he was going home to see you. And if I was any kind of a friend, I'd go with him."

"And you *went?*" she asked incredulously.

"Not voluntarily. But Abby, Jason was drunk. I tried talking to him. Jeez, I even hit him. But come hell or high water, he was going back to Winston. The best I could do was talk him into letting me drive."

Abby levered herself slowly onto a stool on Reed's side of the workbench. "I can't believe that he...that you..."

"I know. It was crazy. The whole thing was crazy." Reed let out a sigh. "We took the long way home, Abby. By the time he'd sobered up enough to take the wheel, we were on the outskirts of Winston, trying like the devil to figure out the best way to handle things."

Abby nodded slowly. "I see. And you figured the best way to handle things was to let Jason hide on the bus while you took the consequences."

Ignoring her sarcasm, Reed shrugged. "We parked in a shady spot on Adelaide and waited for the sheriff to show up. It didn't take long. You know the rest."

"Yes, I know the rest," she said evenly. "You were taken to jail. An hour or so later, Theodora watched Jason sneak off the bus and make his getaway. She wasn't sure how he got back to Jackson in time to come home with the team."

"Hitchhiked," Reed said simply.

"Hitchhiked." Abby tried hard to swallow the anger, the bitterness. "Clean as a whistle, he got away and left you holding the bag."

"Abby, what we did . . . it was for the best."

"Why?" she demanded. "Why was that for the best, Reed? How could he have done it? I thought he was being so noble. Standing by his friend, making excuses for you, when all the time *he* was the one. He never said a word. Not one word."

"I didn't *want* him to tell you. I figured you wouldn't see it the way he and I did. Look at you now, almost eighteen years later, getting all worked up over noth—"

"He didn't deserve you, Reed. You were his friend, and he let you—"

"Abby, I'm the one who chose to do what I did. Jason had worked like a dog for that scholarship, and I didn't believe that one stupid act on his part should've kept him from getting it. My reputation was such that people were willing to believe that *I'd* do something that stupid. And I had nothing to lose."

"Yes, you did. You lost the boxing championship."

"Oh, that."

She stared hard, knowing he wasn't nearly so cavalier as he let on.

Finally he relented. "I have to admit that it made me a little sick but, Abby, I've never regretted it. Not for one minute. He was my friend. I loved him."

For some crazy reason, Abby felt betrayed all over again. Knowing what Jason had done to Reed. What Jason had done to her in their marriage. The tears gathered faster than she could blink them back.

Reed put down the piece of wood he'd been sanding and pulled her off the stool and into his arms. "Abby, please don't cry." He took the shop cloth from his back pocket and gave it to her. "All that was a hundred years ago. It doesn't even matter anymore."

"Yes, it *does* matter. It matters a lot to me. You gave up something you wanted badly, something that was well within your reach, something that would have helped you so much, Reed. You gave it up for someone who didn't even deserve—"

"That's not true," he said. "I gave it up for a friend. Don't ever forget that, Abby. Jason didn't deserve to lose his chance to become a doctor. He couldn't have done without that money. I knew it. He knew it. And I guess Theodora Walsh knew it, too."

"But Reed—"

"Yes, he made mistakes," he said, taking her face gently between his hands. "He made them with me. He made even worse ones with you. And I'm so sorry. But I—I have to believe that with all his faults, he was basically one of the good guys, Abby. And that's why I did it. Besides, he already had the one thing I wanted more than life itself."

"What was that?"

"You."

"Me?"

"Yes. You. Abby, I've been in love with you all my life. Before I even knew what love was, I loved you." His voice was soft and low and Abby could feel the words wrapping slowly around her heart.

"Reed, why didn't you tell me?"

"Because by the time I figured it out, Jason had already claimed you. And it looked very much like you loved him back." He slipped the cloth from her hand. Touching the soft rag to her cheek, Reed smiled. "But, Abby, I'm telling you now. I'm in love with you."

"But...how can you, Reed? I mean...again...after all this time?"

"*Still*. After all this time, I'm in love with you still. Always have been. Always will be."

The tears flowed even faster. She wrapped her arms around his neck and held on tight for support.

"Does this mean there's hope for us?" he asked.

She hugged him closer, but she still couldn't speak, not yet. She supposed she ought to be thinking more clearly. But Abby didn't want to think. She wanted only to savor the sensation of his thumb gently guiding her chin upward. His lips touching hers with such sweetness. She found a little bit of heaven in the manly fingers that stroked her cheek. His other hand circled slowly, sensuously along her spine and down to her hips.

It was just the beginning, she knew, of all that she wanted with Reed. He clearly filled an emptiness and replaced it with an elemental desire, a sense of belonging that she had believed to be forever lost to her. Did she dare to love again? Could she trust again? Oh, she wanted so much to try. But...

"Abby," he murmured huskily against her hair. "Abby, I love you. It feels so good to finally tell you."

The heartfelt declaration sent any protest she might have made spinning into oblivion. It was then that her fears were transformed into sweet wonder. She let go of her reason. Gave way to her dreams. Mesmerizing thoughts melted into liquid impressions, fiery sensations. In a ravaging kiss, she sent word of her own growing need, her own growing passion for Reed.

At that moment he changed.

With a gentle strength, he drew her even closer, until she met with a solid wall of chest. The tip of his tongue teased and plundered, leaving her breathless with pleasure. Somehow in the onslaught, the hem of her skirt began to move higher and higher until Abby could feel his fingers tormenting the flesh of her thighs. In knee-weakening seduction, he cupped her hips and lifted her up to him, pressing her hard against him.

A small gasp pushed past her throat, as a cascade of longing rippled through her. There was no move to go inside his house, not when that would require a parting, however brief, of their bodies. His gaze stayed caressing her face, as he lowered himself slowly, pulling her down along with him until her knees rested on a small round rug near the wall. Abby rather enjoyed the feel of sprinkles of sawdust tingling her skin here and there. The pervasive aroma of wood shavings only served to further shatter her reserve.

His finger traced the silk V neck of her blouse, inciting her flesh as he went. Reed moved the material aside and laid a rough cheek against her breast. There was tender restraint in the hot touch of his mouth against her skin. She cradled his head between her hands and laced her fingers through the rich softness of his hair.

Dazed by the provocative movement of his mouth searing a path from her breast to her throat, she closed her eyes to the tremors that coursed through her limbs. Her breath grew weaker with each erotic caress in the journey to her mouth, where she welcomed another siege on her senses.

Somewhere in the corner of her mind, the clicking sound was noted then dismissed. Her thoughts returned to the bank of hard muscles molding Reed's shoulders and back. She was down to bare skin in her quest to explore the hard planes of his chest, having at some point unbuttoned his shirt enough to slip her hands inside to be warmed by the fire. Letting her fingers glide through the feathery hair, Abby softly moaned her satisfaction.

Reality dawned slowly, swimming its way—a sound here, a shadow there—into her watery consciousness, until Abby realized that she and Reed were no longer alone, until her eyes finally focused on Matthew's form across the room.

His icy stare froze her limbs and brought a startled cry from her throat. In less than an instant, she was pushing herself away from Reed. Clutching the neck of her blouse, Abby struggled to her feet, straightening her skirt as she went.

"Matthew," she said breathlessly, "sweetheart, I thought you were—what are you doing here?"

The contempt, the betrayal, the hurt shot like arrows from his eyes, hitting their mark deep within her. Abby hastily smoothed her hair and swiped at the sawdust on her clothing. When she stepped past Reed, Matthew stiffened, the set of his jaw warning her back.

"Stay away from me."

"Matthew, what is it?" she asked quietly, her voice trembling with embarrassment and a certain shame, for she knew very well what it was. "What's wrong, sw—?"

"What's *wrong?*" He shook his head. "I find you in here with your clothes half...with you looking like this, and you ask me what's *wrong?*" Matthew swallowed bitterly. "How could you do this?" he accused her. "How could you do this to Dad? Don't you care about him? Didn't you love him at all?"

"Of course I did, Matthew, but—"

"We both loved him." Reed levered himself up from the floor and dragged a hand across his forehead.

"Oh, yeah, right," the boy said. "I can see how you really care about him. How can you just forget him like this? How could my own mother act like a...? Well, a mother just doesn't—a *good* mother wouldn't—"

"Matt, stop it," Reed said. "Your mother hasn't—"

"And *you,*" he said hoarsely. "I trusted you of all people. You said you loved my dad. When all you really wanted to do was—how could you use my mother like this? God, don't you have any—" Matthew looked at Abby. "How could you *let* him?"

The words bit into her soul and sickened her. "Oh, Matthew, you don't understand," she pleaded.

"Understand? No, Mom, you're right. I don't understand. I will *never* understand."

"Matt, you're overreacting," Reed said. "Now just try to calm down."

"Calm down? Why should I? Why should I do *anything* you say?" But he did calm down a little. At least, his voice became quieter, the words choking forth, stinging her heart, weighing down her entire body. "You know, my dad died only last year. My *dad,* Reed. The guy you say you and my mother loved so much. And now, this year, you just snap your fingers and she comes run—"

"Son, that isn't true and you know it," Reed said evenly.

"It is true. It *is.*" Matthew's eyes shut tight with pain as he turned and moved to the door. "Now it looks like... I didn't want to lose my mom, too."

"Oh, Matthew." Abby went toward him, but Reed held on to her arm. "Please, try to understand. We never meant to hurt any—"

"Don't," the boy said, his voice trembling with rage. "Just don't even try anymore."

He went out the door and slammed it behind him. Abby wrenched free of Reed's grasp and tried to rub the chill from her arms. "I'll go to him," she said. "I'll go to him and straighten out this whole thing. I'll make him understand. Somehow... I'll... make him."

Reed was beside her again. "Abby, just let him be alone for a while."

"No. I can't do that. He needs me, Reed. After all he's been through, I've got to—"

"Abby, Abby," Reed urged, his hands moving gently up and down her arms, "don't do this to yourself. You haven't done anything wrong."

"I know. But Matthew thinks I have. Don't you see? It's his perception of things, of his life. I can't let him—"

"Think, Abby, think. Don't go off half-cocked the way he did."

"You're right. I need a clear head. I need to think about the best way to help him."

"Good. We'll go someplace and—"

"No, Reed." Abby moved away, trying to think of the best way to tell him. To make him understand. She drew a deep breath and turned to him. "I've got to go back, Reed. To Little Rock. It was wrong of me to take him away from everything and everyone he knows. The house is still on the market. I can—"

"Abby, don't," Reed said. "Don't do this."

"I have to. He's been miserable here and—"

"Matt is going to be miserable anywhere until he reolves this thing. Don't you see?"

She didn't see. Abby didn't see at all. She had been thinking only of herself when she had packed up her children and moved them to Winston, a place where she thought she could feel comfortable, feel alive again. But her children—Matthew at least—had felt no such comfort. She had taken away everything familiar to him. That was wrong. She knew that now. She could see her own selfishness clearly now. And Reed's, too, for trying to make her see things differently.

"I've got to go to my son," she said evenly. "I've got to make some arrange—"

"Don't say it, Abby. Don't say it, because I don't think I can stand to hear it."

"I have to say it. Please," she begged him. "He's my son. He's hurting. I can't just turn my back on him."

Reed came toward her and clasped her arms in a plea for reason. "Abby, you're making way too much of this. Don't run away. Don't let Matt run away. I love you. Matt will come around. He'll understand. You'll see."

She swallowed, wondering if anyone would ever understand anything again. "He's felt abandoned, first by his father and now . . ." Abby covered her face and sobbed. "Do you know how it hurts? My own child believes that I don't care about him, Reed. He's thinks I've abandoned him, too."

"That's not true, damn it. It's not true, and he knows it. Do you hear me? He *knows* you love him," Reed said. "This is a temporary, adolescent overreaction, Abby. And that is all it is. Abby, he knows you. He knows just what buttons to push."

"You're not being fair," Abby said. "Not to him and not to me."

"And God, how well he knows which buttons to push." Reed shook his head in regret. "The one marked Guilt usually gets the best results."

What a harsh, insensitive attitude!

"Reed, you simply don't understand how it was between Matthew and Jason. That boy worshiped his father, followed him around like some puppy always looking, *begging,* for some sign of approval." Abby fought back the tears hard. It seemed such an important thing, not to cry at that moment. "It wasn't that Jason didn't love him. He did. But the man just didn't know how to show it. He simply didn't know what was needed."

"I understand all that," Reed said patiently. "But, Abby, you can't be all things to all people. Not even to your son."

"Maybe I can't," she said. "But I have to do something. That's why I think it's best for us to leave. I hope you'll try to understand." She picked up her sweater and moved to the door.

"Abby?"

Her hand was on the doorknob and yet she couldn't turn it. Not yet.

"I've waited a very long time to be with you," he said softly. "I don't think I can wait any longer. I just don't think I can. So, you have to decide. It's now or never. That's...it."

All the strength went out of her. Abby wished with all her heart that he would take it back. Say he hadn't meant it. She waited a long, agonizing moment. But Reed said nothing.

Abby turned the knob and opened the door.

# Chapter Twelve

Reed heard the gate latch clank once and then again a second or two later. He looked up from his bed of wildflowers and hoped against hope that it would be Abby coming around the corner, Abby appearing in his backyard, Abby armed with an apology. A plea. Something.

It wasn't Abby.

It was Matthew, dressed in a T-shirt and jeans and slouching his way toward the wisteria arbor. Reed let out the breath he'd been holding and went back to cutting the last hardy blooms of the season. A week had passed and no word. That said something, he reasoned. He wasn't sure what it said, but it damned sure said something.

"It was Mom, wasn't it?"

The kid was standing right beside him now. But Reed ignored him.

"That person you told me about," Matthew explained further, "the special girl who loved somebody else."

Keep cutting, Reed told himself. Snip this one, snip that one. And maybe he'll go away.

"It was Mom, wasn't it?"

"Matt, I don't want to talk about this." Reed picked up the full basket of flowers and moved to the patio table.

"Yeah?" The boy dogged his steps all the way. "Well, ain't *that* a kick in the pants."

Funny, the kid didn't *look* like Ben Mackintosh.

"You're after us guys to talk all the time, to tell you what's bothering us," Matthew said. "But when it's your turn, it's none of our business, is that it?"

"No," Reed said, "that isn't it. It's just that all that is old news. Doesn't mean a thing anymore, what happened when I was your age."

"Yeah, well, it still bothers you, doesn't it? I mean this person you told me about and how she loved somebody else. You still think about it, don't you? It probably ruined your senior year, didn't it?"

"Gee, Matt, I think it might have affected a little more than my senior year," Reed said dryly, a little amused, a lot sad.

Hell, whatever he had felt for Abby had affected his entire outlook on life, the way he thought about the world. The way he thought about himself. And all those nights he had lain awake thinking about her. God, how he had thought about her back then. Almost as much as he thought about her now.

Still, Reed didn't think he ought to have to take this from a smart mouthed kid who didn't know anything about anything. That same kid was eyeing him now, waiting for an answer. Reed wondered if he could possibly get him into the subject of tables.

"Well?" Matthew demanded.

Reed cleared his throat. He could just make out the tip of a bright red bow moving along the top of his privacy fence. Henrietta Walsh was out early, he noted. A morning appearance truly meant that the dog days of summer had passed and autumn was on its way.

Matthew snorted. "What's the deal, Reed? You're always telling us to open up. Be honest. Well, what about you? Can't you take the heat?"

"All right, all right. Yes, it was your mother. Damn if you're not just as hardheaded as she is." The kid seemed pleased by the comment. Proud, even. "Now, do you mind if we go inside before the whole town..." Reed let out a sigh. "Let's continue this in the house."

"No kidding? Mom?" Matthew followed him into the kitchen. Reed had to gesture blatantly to remind him to close the door. "Oh. Right. Anyway, you were...I mean...did you love her or somethin'?"

"I thought the sun rose and set with her." Reed helped himself to a glass of water and leaned against the countertop.

"No kidding." Matthew shook his head and his voice became quiet. "Wow. What did she think? I mean, did she feel the same way?"

"Obviously not, since she married your father."

"Oh, yeah, right." Still, Matthew couldn't seem to leave the subject alone. "Well, did she even know that you...I mean, how you felt and stuff?"

"Did she know how I felt?" Reed drew a bolstering breath. He wasn't having a very good time remembering this. "I took great pains to keep her and everyone else from finding out."

"But why? Why didn't you say somethin'?"

"You know, I really don't know why I never said anything. To tell you the truth, it isn't something I like to think much about." Reed took his glass to the table and sat. "I've done a lot of stupid things in my life. Especially where your mother is concerned."

"You should've been honest," Matthew suggested firmly.

"Yeah. But I couldn't. For several reasons, the main one being that your dad was my best friend—he really *was* my best friend, Matt. And he loved her. There was no way I would have tried to take Abby from him." Reed smiled wryly. "Then there was the very large doubt that I *could* have taken her away. It isn't unlike the situation you're in. Except that I think your chances are probably better than mine were."

"Whadda ya mean?"

"You and Carrie Alexander. And Frankie."

Matthew's mouth dropped open and he quickly shut it again. "No, man, you got it all wrong," he said, his cheeks coloring slightly. "That's no big deal."

"Right." Obviously it had the makings of a very big deal.

"Anyway, that's different."

"Oh? How is it different?"

"Well, I'm almost fifteen, and you're old . . . er. And if I really liked someone—and I'm not sayin' I do—I'd probably figure out a way to tell 'em. At least, before I turned thirty."

"I hope you do. You'll save yourself a lot of trouble."

Matthew said nothing. The two of them sat in silence for a few minutes. Reed wondered if the kid was even going to mention what had happened the week before in the workshop. If he didn't, Reed figured that he himself would have to bring it up. There were things that needed to be said, regardless of what happened with Abby.

"Reed?"

"Yeah?" he said, annoyed with himself and the rest of the world that things had come to this. Sad that he couldn't seem to find the will or the wherewithal to do anything about it. "What is it, son?"

"I guess I need to apologize for . . . you know . . . the stuff I said to you and Mom . . . that time." Matthew cleared his throat, but it didn't seem to relieve his discomfort. "I already talked to Mom and . . ."

"She forgave you."

"Yeah. But she said some stuff about how she understood how I felt and...stuff, but that I didn't have the right to hurt her the way I did."

"She's right about—"

"Just let me get this out, would you please?"

Reed clammed up and gave Matthew the go-ahead.

"She said she had the right to look for someone to spend the rest of her life with. That someday, Molly and I would be gone and if it wasn't you, then it would probably be somebody else."

"She did? Abby said that?" Good Lord, did she already have someone waiting in the wings? "Did she say anything else?"

"Well, we talked about my dad some."

"Good. I'm glad you did, because you seem to be carrying around some bad feelings about you and him."

"Mom said maybe I should talk to you because maybe you'd understand better than she did. Us both being guys and all."

Oh, really. Reed distinctly remembered her accusing him of not understanding at all. She was a slick one, that Abby. He could tell right now that he was going to have to watch that woman every minute for the rest of his life. Meanwhile, here was Matt waiting for some kind of advice...reassurance...whatever. The only thing to do was jump in with both feet and see what happened.

"You know, Matt, I was about your age when I lost my mother," he said easily, as if his heart no longer ached every time he thought about her. "For the longest time, I couldn't deal with that. Anyhow, it's safe to say that I wasn't the easiest person to get along with."

"Kinda like me," Matthew said.

Reed waved the notion away. "I had it all over you when it came to belligerence. But finally, after years of being in a constant state of war, well, one day my father grabbed me and more or less told me how the cow ate the cabbage."

Matthew waited, probably wondering what the hell all this had to do with him and his own father. Reed had begun to wonder that, too. He'd begun to wonder if he was completely blowing it.

He got up for more water. "Dad told me that he was really sorry that my mother was gone, but that those were the breaks in life and we would just have to do the best we could and live with it."

"Sounds like a pretty mean thing to say, if you ask me."

Reed smiled. "At the time, I thought it was a brutal thing to say. But it did get my attention. Made me start thinking differently about things. To be honest, I think it's good advice for you, too."

The boy shifted in his chair. "Why do you say that?"

"Obviously you think your dad didn't spend enough time with you. Maybe you think that meant that he didn't care about you. That he didn't love you. And that you could never measure up. And I'm sure you've felt hurt, thinking that."

Matthew swallowed. "Yeah, I have, but—"

"About the only thing I can say to you is what my father told me," Reed said as gently as he knew how. "If you didn't get what you wanted or needed from Jason, you'll just have to grow up and carry on with those things that he did give you. Live with it, in other words—and I don't mean that in any cruel sense."

Matthew sighed, making it clear that he was uncomfortable listening to what was being said.

Reed came close and put a hand on the boy's shoulder. "It's a sad fact that some men make lousy fathers, Matt. Whether it's because they're too young or too selfish, too ignorant or too irresponsible, some guys just never learn how to do it right. And if that's what you think of your dad, I can't argue, because I wasn't there. Only you can judge what kind of father he was to you." Reed sat at the table again, but he didn't take his eyes off Matthew. "But, son, don't ever think for one minute that he didn't care. Because he did. I know that because I was there the first time he held you. A man's tears don't lie."

"Dad cried?"

"Oh, yes," Reed assured him. "That same day he went out and got a Razorback football helmet. Of course, your mother wouldn't let him put it on that shiny little head of yours." Matthew actually laughed. It was a rather pleasant sound that reminded Reed so much of Jason and the good times they had shared. "Yes, your dad loved you," Reed said after a few moments of remembering. "Maybe his problem was that he didn't get to live long enough to show you, to let you know what a great kid you are."

Matthew's expression mellowed even more as he nodded and looked away. "Thanks. Mom said pretty much the same thing you're telling me."

"Oh. Well, good." Reed would bet that Abby had said it a hundred times better than he had. That's the kind of woman she was. She knew just the right things to say. She knew how to make people feel good. She always had.

"What do you think's going to happen now?" Matthew said. "With you and Mom—if it's okay for me to ask. How do you think she feels now?"

"I don't know," Reed said. "Lately we haven't talked much about feelings."

"Well, maybe you should go and see her."

"Why? Is she unhappy?"

"She isn't moping around or anything like that—Mom doesn't do stuff like that—but I think she misses you. Gets a little quiet sometimes. And yesterday, when I told her I was going to buy a snake, she just nodded. I don't think she was listening. She does that a lot."

Reed was almost afraid to be encouraged.

"So, how would you feel, Matt, if your mother and I did get together?"

Matthew kept his gaze on the table. "I'm not saying it would be easy for me, because it wouldn't. But I want Mom to be happy. And if you're what makes her happy..." The boy shrugged and met Reed's eyes. "Then go for it."

It wasn't the highest recommendation Reed had ever received. Still, he wasn't about to wait around for something better. Trouble was, he no longer *knew* if he was what made Abby happy. In any case, he appreciated her son's endorsement.

"Thanks. I'll keep that in mind." Matthew hadn't even mentioned moving back to Little Rock. Reed couldn't bring himself to ask. Mainly because he didn't think he could stomach the answer.

After another awkward moment, the boy cleared his throat and got up to go. "Mr. Mackintosh in his office, you think?"

Reed nodded. "Every Saturday morning, like clockwork."

"Uh-huh. Guess I should apologize to him, too. Then my mom's got some stuff for me to do." Matthew's hand curled around the doorknob before he turned to Reed again. "Well, just so you know... if you were to come over tonight, say around eight-thirty... I probably wouldn't even be there."

# Chapter Thirteen

"*In Dublin's fair city, where girls are so pretty, I first set my eyes on sweet Molly Malone. . . .*"

Holding her place in the book, Abby sat up on Molly's bed and listened. Someone was singing outside. "Molly, do you hear that?" The rich—and suspiciously familiar—male voice was getting louder.

"*As she wheeled her wheelbarrow through streets broad and narrow, crying, 'Cockles and mussels! Alive, alive oh!'*"

"It's Reed!" her daughter squealed. "Mama, it's Reed!" Molly hopped out of bed and went straight to the window. Abby put down the book and followed, her heart beating perceptibly, wonderfully, faster.

"*'Alive, alive oh. Alive, alive oh'. Crying 'Cockles and mussels, alive, alive oh!'*"

In the twilight, Reed stood on the lawn and began another chorus. From their perch at the window above him, Abby drew the sheer curtains aside and listened, letting the pleasing timbre of his voice curve her mouth with deep satisfaction.

She was certain he could be heard all over the neighborhood, which only served to increase her amusement. Molly's, too, she noted, when her daughter began clapping her hands and cheering before the man had finished his last "alive, alive oh," which he drew out to tremulous and totally unnecessary length.

Reed received further applause and even a whistle from several people who had interrupted their evening stroll along the avenue to witness his performance. He took full advantage of the audience, bowing several times and generally hamming it up, before allowing them to continue on their way.

Finally he turned and looked up to the window again. "Good evening, ladies," he said with the slightest wave of his hand.

Abby smiled. "What are you doing here, Reed Mackintosh?"

"Isn't it obvious? I came to serenade Molly and...maybe have a word with you."

"Reed, could you come up and read me a story?" Molly called down to him.

"Sure, if it's all right with your mother."

It wasn't all right. Tonight Abby so much wanted him all to herself. "Of course it's all right," she said. "Then...we'll talk."

He seemed pleased.

She drew Molly away from the window and put her into bed. "Reed will be up in a minute." She kissed her daughter good-night. "Sweet dreams."

Abby hurried to her room to run a brush through her hair and assess her appearance in the mirror. Not too bad, she decided, when she considered the week she'd spent brooding. She tucked her blouse inside her slacks and touched a hint of perfume to her neck. Switching off the light, she could hear Reed's low voice already well into *The Best Nest,* one of Molly's favorites.

When he joined her downstairs in the kitchen, Abby had hardly arrived herself. There were no formalities, no prelude to intimacy, not even any conversation. Reed simply came to her, took the coffee canister from her hands and set it aside before pulling her into his arms for a long and thoroughly enjoyable kiss. A kiss that sent her nerves clamoring for answers to all kinds of questions.

Something was definitely afoot, she decided, holding on to Reed for support. "Well, that didn't take long," she said, relaxing against his chest. "The story, I mean."

"When I have to, I can paraphrase like crazy."

She giggled into his shoulder and then sighed. "Would you like some coffee?"

"I'd love some coffee."

She bit her lip nervously. "I'll make it," she said, letting go to slip between him and the table.

"Abby, wait."

"Change your mind?"

"No. But I need to... Abby, I did a very unwise thing last time we talked."

"Oh? What was that?"

"I gave you an ultimatum—a stupid and totally insane ultimatum."

She stared at the floor and prayed that he had come to make things right again. "Yes, you did. So what are you going to do about it?"

"Can you forget I ever said it?" he ventured huskily.

Abby smiled, tracing the strong line of his jaw with her finger. "Not a chance. I intend to bring it up at least twice a year for the rest of our lives."

Reed relaxed visibly and let out a breath. "That must mean that you plan for us to live at least part of our lives together."

"Oh, I don't know," Abby teased. "Maybe in close proximity."

"Come here, you," he muttered, and crushed her against him. She gladly accepted the apology and then the promise in his kiss. Her forgiveness went unspoken, but she was certain he knew there was little that she could deny him.

"I love you, Reed," she whispered. How could she not love a man whose chest swelled with such joy at the simple confession she'd made. Whose voice trembled with his own throaty plea.

"Don't ever stop, Abby. Please. Because I won't. I can't. I'll go along with whatever you decide. If you move back to Little Rock, I'll go with you. If you don't want me there, I'll visit whenever you'll let me." His lips sent an urgent whisper to her cheek. "Just don't say we can't be together."

Abby could feel her own heart beginning to swell. "I won't say that. I couldn't." She held his face in her hands and stroked him. "Things are better around here. Matthew and I have talked. A lot. I thought about everything you said—that we can't run away anymore. You were right. If I'd been thinking clearly..." Abby shrugged her own remorse. "Anyway, he seems to be coming around."

"I know. He paid me a visit this morning to apologize. Even gave us his blessing, in a manner of speaking. I'm sure it took a lot of courage, considering how we left things a week ago."

Abby smiled her pride, her joy. She left him with a fleeting kiss and all but floated to the sink to make the coffee, while Reed set out the cream and looked through the cabinets for sugar. He didn't ask and she didn't tell him where it was, mainly because she thoroughly enjoyed watching him make himself at home. He finally located the sugar bowl and set it on the table beside the creamer.

"This is nice," she said softly, coming to him again. "Very nice."

"What's that?"

"Having you here. You must know it'll be all over town before midnight that I've gone and trapped the most handsome—not to mention the sexiest—man in the state right here in my kitchen."

Reed groaned at her teasing prediction.

Abby let her fingers play in the soft hair at his nape. "Don't try to tell me you're not the least bit thrilled by the reputation you have."

"Not in the least," he muttered.

"Oh, I'm sure you've heard it all a thousand times," she said Southern-style, then sighed, racking her brain to remember just the way Mavis had put it. "First, you've got your big green eyes, a chin to die for and oh, yes, that cute little lopsided grin. Oh, and just all sorts of things to make a girl go limp."

Abby closed her eyes and let herself do that very thing against Reed's chest. On impact, she heard a distinct male groan. After that, Reed kept his own end up admirably. "Well, with all that," he said with a bit of strain as he held her, "what else could a woman want?"

Her sigh was wistful. "Oh, I don't know," she said, looking up at him. "But a couple of chili dogs wouldn't hurt."

"Mom, are you all right?" Alarm laced the words as Matthew hurried into the kitchen.

Abby scrambled back to an upright position and straightened her clothing. "Oh...I...we..."

"She's fine," Reed said. "Just got a little weak in the knees for a minute there. Probably her diet. All those chili dogs, you know."

Matthew's mouth dropped open. "I've noticed that. She tells me all the time, 'the four food groups, Matthew, the four food groups.' But does she ever follow her own advice? No. You can't tell her anything because she won't lis—" He stopped and bit his lip. "Jeez, I'm beginning to sound like her."

"I think you sound exactly like her," Reed said.

"Oh, man, I gotta work on that."

"Say, aren't you supposed to be somewhere?" Reed asked, glancing at his watch.

Matthew nodded. "Yeah, but a guy's gotta eat once in a while."

"Well, here," Reed said, reaching for his wallet. "Try a pepperoni pizza. As far as I know, it involves at least three of the food groups." He handed Matthew a bill. "At least, I think it does."

"Hey, if you want to get rid of me in style," Matthew teased, "you could always spring for a movie, too."

"Don't push your luck," Reed said. "If you can get pizza and a movie for twenty bucks, then be my guest."

"Thanks," Matthew said, genuinely pleased, and then he seemed hesitant. "I— I don't suppose you guys'll want to go with us or anything."

"Oh, I don't think Molly's quite up to it," Abby said. "If I know her, she's already asleep."

"Yeah, thanks for the offer, but we'll pass on the pizza and maybe just go for a short walk, if you don't mind staying with your sister until we get back."

All in all, it sounded like heaven to Abby. "Uh, would you mind terribly, son?"

"Nah. Go ahead."

"If Molly wakes up, try to be patient with her and—"

Matthew clearly looked insulted. "Don't worry, I can handle it."

"I know, Matthew. I know you can," Abby said. "We won't be gone long."

"We'll be back before dawn," Reed added.

"Hey, wai—"

"Just kidding." Reed scooted Abby out the door and down the steps.

She put her hand in his, and they walked for several blocks in the moonlight. Reed shared with her the dreams he had dreamed through the years without her. Abby told him a few of her own expectations, her triumphs, her losses. She talked about Jason's affair and what it had meant to her and their marriage. She made a promise to Reed to try very hard to lay it to rest, to try to forget the bitterness and concentrate on the good that Jason had brought to her life, namely her children. Now she wanted only to remember the special love she and Jason and Reed had shared. A love that had brought her full circle back to Winston . . . and Reed.

Every now and then along the way, Reed stopped her and held her close, giving her the strength she needed to forgive, the faith she needed to hope again. The ease with which she was able to speak about the past surprised her, until she realized that her comfort came from telling it all to the dearest friend she had ever known.

Under a street lamp at the corner of Melrose and May, he stopped once more and kissed her, letting her know his constant devotion. His thrilling intentions. He rested his rough cheek alongside her softer one in a heartfelt invitation. "Marry me, Abby?"

The words cascaded over her. Abby felt weak with her own desire. "I want that, Reed. I want that very much."

"Soon?"

Abby smiled her total agreement. "Soon."

"I've known you all my life," he said. "But in so many ways, we're just beginning."

A fanciful autumn breeze blew gently across her loving eyes and riffled through her hair. "Let's go home," she whispered. "Let's go home and begin."

* * * * *

# Silhouette ROMANCE™

## COMING NEXT MONTH

**#1084 MAKE ROOM FOR BABY—Kristin Morgan**
*Bundles of Joy*
Once, Camille Boudreaux and Bram Delcambre dreamed of
marriage—until betrayal tore them apart. But with a new baby
about to join them together as a family, would their love get a
second chance?

**#1085 DADDY LESSONS—Stella Bagwell**
*Fabulous Fathers*
Joe McCann was about to fire Savanna Starr until he saw her skill
at child rearing. Would helping this single dad raise his teenage
daughter lead to a new job—as his wife?

**#1086 WILDCAT WEDDING—Patricia Thayer**
*Wranglers and Lace*
Nothing would get between Jessie Burke and her ranch. Not even
dynamic oilman Brett Murdock. But Brett had more on his mind
than Jessie's land. He wanted Jessie—for life.

**#1087 HIS ACCIDENTAL ANGEL—Sandra Paul**
*Spellbound*
Bree Smith was supposed to teach cynical Devlin Hunt about
love—not fall for the handsome bachelor! What chance did an
angel like her have with a man who didn't believe in miracles?

**#1088 BELATED BRIDE—Charlotte Moore**
Karen Haig had left her hometown a jilted bride years ago. Now she
was back—and her former fiancé Seth Bjornson had a plan to make
her stay. But could she trust her heart to Seth again?

**#1089 A CONVENIENT ARRANGEMENT—Judith Janeway**
*Debut Author*
Jo Barnett might be sharing a home with Alex MacHail but she
wasn't about to share her life with him. Then Alex introduced
her to his adorable little boy, and Jo found herself falling for father
and son.

# Take 4 bestselling love stories FREE

## Plus get a FREE surprise gift!

**Continuing in May from**

**by**
**Carolyn Zane**

When twin sisters trade places, mischief, mayhem and romance are sure to follow!

You met Erica in UNWILLING WIFE (SR#1063). Now Emily gets a chance to find her perfect man in:

**WEEKEND WIFE (SR#1082)**

Tyler Newroth needs a wife—just for the weekend. And kindhearted Emily Brant can't tell him no. But she soon finds herself wishing this temporary marriage was for real!

Don't miss this wonderful continuation of the SISTER SWITCH series. Available in May—only from

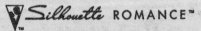

SSD2

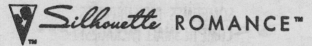

# is proud to present

The spirit of the West—and the magic of romance... Saddle up and get ready to fall in love Western-style with WRANGLERS & LACE. Look for the second book this June:

## Wildcat Wedding
### by Patricia Thayer

Nothing would get between Jessie Burke and her ranch. Not even dynamic oilman Brett Murdock. But Brett had more on his mind than Jessie's land. He wanted Jessie—for life.

**Wranglers & Lace:** Hard to tame—impossible to resist—these cowboys meet their match.

SL-2

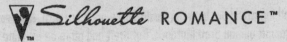

## Announcing
# the New Pages & Privileges™ Program
## from Harlequin® and Silhouette®

### Get All This FREE
### With Just One Proof-of-Purchase!

- **FREE Travel Service** with the guaranteed lowest available airfares plus 5% cash back on every ticket

- **FREE Hotel Discounts** of up to 60% off at leading hotels in the U.S., Canada and Europe

- **FREE Petite Parfumerie** collection (a $50 Retail value)

- **FREE $25 Travel Voucher** to use on any ticket on any airline booked through our Travel Service

- **FREE Insider Tips Letter** full of fascinating information and hot sneak previews of upcoming books

- **FREE Mystery Gift** (if you enroll before May 31/95)

And there are more great gifts and benefits to come!
Enroll today and become Privileged!

(see insert for details)

---

# PROOF-OF-PURCHASE

Offer expires October 31, 1996                    SR-PP1